GRACE'S COTTAGE

Jennifer is a small-town girl living with, and caring for, her invalid mother and wayward sister. Sam is an architect from the big city, brooding over a dark secret from his past. When Sam visits the café where Jennifer works, she is less than impressed with his brusque manner. However, as a series of events throws them together, their growing attraction is undeniable. Can the two of them overcome the considerable difficulties that stand in the way of their happiness together, or will they be forced to go their separate ways?

NOELENE JENKINSON

GRACE'S COTTAGE

Complete and Unabridged

LINFORD
Leicester

First published in Great Britain

First Linford Edition
published 2014

A catalogue record for this book is available
from the British Library.

ISBN 978–1–4448–2007–2

Published by
F. A. Thorpe (Publishing)
Anstey, Leicestershire

Set by Words & Graphics Ltd.
Anstey, Leicestershire
Printed and bound in Great Britain by
T. J. International Ltd., Padstow, Cornwall

This book is printed on acid-free paper

1

Jennifer Hale's long fair hair fluttered out behind her as she cycled hard against the stiff spring breeze sweeping down Bundilla's sleepy Main Street.

Her wicker basket gave a dull rattle as she hit a pothole. She cringed, hoping the contents of the box survived as she turned the corner and headed along Creek Street. The low banks of the tiny burbling waterway were lined with bracken and scrambling native plants. Golden wattles glowed through the bush in the last slanting rays of light before sunset.

Halfway along, Jennifer steered her beloved blue bike into the driveway along one side of a block of rental flats. She shared Number Three with her youngest sibling and only sister, Rachel, and their reserved mother, Rose. Thinking of her sister, Jennifer suspected her great day at Sue's café where she worked on weekends was about to plummet. Conversations with belligerent Rachel were never easy and often challenging. Jennifer felt a fierce sense of responsibility while their vulnerable mother fully recovered but Rachel defied any advice. All of them were affected by the late Reverend Thomas Hale's oppression in their lives.

She propped her bike in its usual place against the brick wall in the empty carport. Jennifer preferred her bicycle, with its comfortable padded leather seat. Treadly was her pride and joy because she wouldn't allow herself the indulgence of a car until she had saved toward her dream. Or, more accurately, her mother's.

Rose Hale, who had moved with her minister husband every few years to another parish calling in yet another church manse, had once wistfully confided her dream of living in her own home. So her oldest daughter was trying to make it happen. For all of them. But mostly to return peace to her mother's life. Although Rose was only in her sixties and physically fit, she endured bouts of prolonged nervous depression. A legacy of her husband's harsh temperament, as was Rachel's rebellion. So Jennifer was striving to make her mother's nostalgia for the happy cottage home of her childhood come true.

She carefully scooped up the cardboard container of quiche from the basket along with three generous slices of lemon cheesecake — café leftovers they would reheat for dinner — slung her bag over her shoulder, and went inside.

'Hey, Mum.' She held the box aloft as she bent to plant an affectionate kiss on her mother's forehead, receiving a gentle smile in return. Judging by the light flush on her pale cheeks, brushed hair, and cotton dress and cardigan she wore instead of the dressing gown when Jennifer left for work this morning, she looked brighter.

'Did you get outside today in the sun?' she asked hopefully.

'For a while.'

Rose devotedly tended their small patch of garden behind the flat, nurturing vegetables, her green thumb evident in the healthy lushness of everything horticultural she touched. On the rare occasion she had a good day — or, more encouraging still, a run of them — she also wandered around to potter in the manse garden. The half acre around the large white weatherboard house that had been their former temporary home like all the others for a few years, had become Rose's sanctuary and salvation. Therapy. A tonic no medicine could achieve.

Jennifer eyed the girl seated alongside her mother on the sofa, her short dark hair chopped into its latest spiky coloured arrangement. 'Hey, Sis.' She made the gesture but didn't expect a response.

Bent in concentration as she painted her nails a hectic shade of purple, Rachel grunted but didn't look up. Their three other siblings, all brothers, had long since moved away to work and study elsewhere.

'Ta-da!' Jennifer placed the box on the kitchen counter. 'Dinner.'

Rachel looked across and sneered as her sister opened it to reveal the contents. 'Quiche is so last century. Baby food. Eggs and milk. You know I hate it.'

'Sue Parker's homemade recipes are the best in town.' Jennifer supported her chef and boss.

Apart from the cans of soft drink that lined the refrigerator door shelves, Jennifer doubted her sister had eaten properly all day or prepared anything for their mother. Still, without bothering to wait for the others, her ungrateful sibling grabbed a fork and helped herself to a large cold serving, then sat down on the sagging sofa and ate it in her usual sullen mood, not talking, watching television as though no one else existed.

Jennifer eyed the shabby furniture with frustration. She had tried to improve its appearance with cheap slipcovers and second-hand cushions from thrift shops, but it was still uncomfortable. As she heated the remaining food and set out plates, cutlery and a jar of homemade relish on the table, Jennifer ignored Rachel's ingratitude, pushing through her disappointment yet again, and addressed her mother.

'You should see the menu Sue's slaved over all day for Ben Fisher's eightieth birthday tonight. Pork roast and heaps of crackling. The smell that wafted through the café from the kitchen.' She rolled her eyes. 'Asparagus and cheese sauce, potato bake. And of course great bowls of mixture ready-prepared for her signature crêpes.'

'And charges the earth for it, too,' Rachel sniped.

'Sue buys only the best and freshest local produce.' Jennifer praised her talented industrious boss. 'Customers appreciate that these days and are prepared to pay for quality.'

'Well I think it's a rip-off and they're suckers.'

Rachel pointed the remote at the television, constantly changing channels, restless and lacking concentration. Not surprising when you considered all the sugar the girl consumed in a day. Jennifer shook her head and released a quiet sigh as she eased off the comfortable flat court shoes she wore for work and glanced around the messy flat. She'd barely had time for the washing and ironing early this morning. It was supposed to be Rachel's turn to clean. Clearly not, for the place was still cluttered, if not worse than when she left.

Jennifer perched on the end of the sofa, swinging one of her long legs to and fro. 'Get that job application done?'

Rachel stifled a yawn. 'Didn't have time. Boomer came around.'

Jennifer cringed at the mention of her sister's latest boyfriend. Not the smartest choice. Then she felt uncharitable for her prejudice just because he wore black and displayed tattoos. 'How do you expect to pay your half of the rent if you don't get yourself another job?' she hinted.

'Not my fault, the long hours they expected me to work.' Rachel sounded injured. 'Anyway, why the panic? You're the crazy workaholic with two jobs.' She tilted one shoulder in an insolent shrug. 'We have plenty of money coming in.'

'I'm working for a purpose. Not to support you,' Jennifer snapped back, growing impatient.

'Yeah. Your stupid dream to buy a house. As if. Like that's ever going to happen.'

'I'm working so it does happen. If you don't start paying your way, Rachel, you can start thinking about leaving.'

As much as she felt responsible for her sister, and eviction was merely a threat, it would be far less stressful for all of them if Rachel could straighten out her life. Maybe fending for herself would prove the wakeup call she needed.

Rachel scoffed. 'You wouldn't. I'm your little sister. You promised Father you would take care of me.' She glanced across at their bemused mother staring into space. 'Mum can't.'

Jennifer cringed that she spoke so disrespectfully in front of her. 'At our age, it's no one's responsibility to take care of us. We're adults, Rachel. We're supposed to make our own way in the world.'

'Goody goody Jennifer wouldn't break a promise, would she?' She met her oldest sibling with a cold stare of challenge.

'Last warning, Rachel,' Jennifer said quietly. 'Get a job.'

'I don't have any skills.'

'And whose fault is that? If you don't educate yourself, it won't happen.'

'I can't study and work at the same time,' Rachel protested.

'Of course you can.'

'I'm not smart like you.' She folded her arms and turned away.

'That's a cop-out and you know it. You just need to try.'

'Okay for you to talk. It comes easy to you.'

Jennifer took a deep breath for a pause in yet another pointless argument as much as to calm her exasperation. 'You could work during the day and study at night online.' No response. 'I'll help.' She tried to sound positive and encouraging. When she would find the time, was a question with no answer. Working two jobs, confronting Rachel on a daily basis, and coping with an unwell mother meant her life was already stretched to the limit.

'How?' Rachel eventually responded with vague interest.

Foolish perhaps, but Jennifer grasped at a thread of hope for the girl. 'Read your assignments. Swap ideas. You can do it.'

'Study costs money,' she scowled.

'That's why you get a job.' Jennifer plastered a cheesy grin on her face and tried to lighten their disagreement. At the sound of a throbbing motorbike engine outside, she frowned. 'I thought you saw Boomer already today.'

Rachel avoided her gaze and squirmed. 'We're going out again.'

'Where in Bundilla at this time of night?' Jennifer grew suspicious.

Rachel shrugged. 'Dunno. We'll think of somewhere. Saturday nights suck in small towns.'

As the girl heaved herself off the sofa, Jennifer suggested, 'Take a coat. Nights are still chilly.' She would be exposed to the elements on the bike. 'Don't forget early service together tomorrow morning at St. Luke's.' Jennifer always hinted for Rachel to return at a decent hour.

'I might need to sleep in if I have a great night,' she smirked.

Jennifer shuddered to think what that meant. 'Then get Boomer to bring you home early.'

Rachel rolled her eyes. 'Not my fault if the only decent entertainment on weekends is miles away from this dump.'

She grew more dissatisfied with every passing week. Boomer's influence, no doubt, but her sister was twenty-one now and, while Jennifer might tactfully advise, she couldn't stop her from going out and doing whatever she chose. Their mother had limited strength to discipline these days.

'By the way,' said Rachel, turning as she headed for the door, 'that old duck Grace Evans died.'

'Oh!' Jennifer knew a moment's genuine distress. 'The spinster from Market Lane?'

'Boomer was driving past on his motorbike and saw the ambulance out the front of her cottage.' Rachel looked rather smug to be imparting such sad news. 'He stopped and asked what was happening.'

Boomer's interest was probably in casing out the place, Jennifer thought. It would be empty now if a person had theft in mind. She chided herself for thinking so poorly of him. Everyone had some redeeming features. Boomer's were just buried deeper than most.

'Mel and Barbara Keats were there.'

'At Grace's cottage? What would they have to do with her?' Jennifer frowned.

Rachel shrugged. 'Dunno, but Boomer said the younger bloke was really upset.'

'Who?'

'Boomer didn't recognise him.'

Rose scowled as if trying to remember. 'I think there was a son,' she said quietly into the brief silence. 'He lives in Melbourne.'

Jennifer raised her eyebrows. 'I didn't know Mel and Barbara Keats had any children.'

Ambitious Mel Keats owned a successful construction company and was wealthy from his efforts. He and wife Barbara were the unofficial elite in the local small community and lived in an imposing home on their estate, Melville Park, amid acres of sprawling grounds on the edge of town. It harmonized with other large properties out that way, running horse studs or sheep, a few exploiting the niche tourism market of bed and breakfasts in the beautiful surrounding hills.

Jennifer looked puzzled. 'Grace must have meant something to the Keats family then. Being a similar age, perhaps they're old friends. Death is sad and final enough but it's hard to fathom that even an unmarried woman like Grace Evans didn't have other family somewhere. Even harder to imagine such a quiet lady having anything in common with the Keats family.'

'Maybe. Don't really care, actually,' Rachel said, leaving her empty plate on the kitchen bench for someone else to clean up. 'Gotta go. Don't wait up,' was her cheeky retort as she left.

Jennifer breathed a guilty sigh of relief that she and mother would eat companionably alone at the small round second-hand dining table with its four mismatched chairs. 'Grace's cottage is probably a renovator's dream,' she mused. On a thought, she asked her mother, 'Did you ever go and do a parish home visit to her while she was alive?'

'No, dear,' Rose murmured. 'She wasn't our church.'

'An elderly lady like that living alone all these years and probably on a pension wouldn't have been able to afford much upkeep. I wonder what it's like inside?' Jennifer rose from the table, gathered their plates to rinse them in the sink, and transfered the cheesecake onto dessert plates. 'I only knew her for her regular visit to the café for lunch every Friday. Seemed to be her shopping day. She always carried bags.' Jennifer chatted on, unsure if her mother was listening or daydreaming. She never knew how much she absorbed, but she was gradually becoming more aware these days. 'She always had the soup of the day and Devonshire tea. She seemed to be a private person. Not so much shy as reserved. A true gentlewoman of her era. It was difficult trying to make conversation with her though.' Jennifer set their dishes on the table and sat down opposite her mother again. 'She usually just smiled and didn't comment.'

Later on, she said, 'I wonder what will happen to her lovely little cottage tucked away in that leafy garden?' She felt heartless for the direction of her thoughts. Grace Evans was barely cold and she was coveting her home.

'Life reveals all in time, dear,' Rose ventured, always a woman of few words and often prophetic despite her inertia.

Jennifer's longing surfaced again and she decided to browse through her stack of precious home decorating magazines later when her mother retired early for the night. Long sleeps were a necessity in her recovery and, Jennifer also suspected, an escape from the reality of unwanted memories. She had refused to be prescribed any drugs, so it was only time that would see her improve.

Jennifer and Rose shared a twin room mainly because Jennifer wanted to be close for her mother. In months past, she had been inclined to have nightmares and wander. Besides, it made more sense that neither of them should be disturbed when Rachel came blundering home in the early morning hours most nights of the week. Especially since Boomer's arrival on the scene. For her sister's sake, Jennifer hoped it didn't last.

Having it drummed into them by their father not to place emphasis on material possessions, the cramped flat was at least a roof over their heads since he died, and the family had been obliged to vacate the church-owned manse. Jennifer tolerated their present humble accommodation as a temporary home but, eventually, as Rachel had so scathingly criticised, she had other plans. Okay, so maybe it was a pipe dream, but it was one she clung to every day if it meant giving her mother a more settled contented life. She'd certainly not known it during decades of a miserable marriage.

As her brain bubbled with possibilities for a home of their own, Jennifer worried about Rachel and her rough boyfriend. Well, he looked rough. Maybe he was a gentle giant. She must talk to David again. Her sister's life was spinning out of control and, although she hurt everyone around her, Jennifer didn't want to see her crash. Vicar David Ormond had been Jennifer's strength after Thomas Hale died a year ago. Wilful Rachel had gone wild with freedom. Jennifer worried since, with their mother's illness, any responsibility for watching out for her welfare fell to her. She found it difficult and frustrating trying to guide a young sibling when she rejected any help.

Jennifer grew absorbed in the home furnishing pages of her magazines for shoestring renovation ideas. Finally she yielded to weariness just before midnight. Still no sign of Rachel. Luckily her shift didn't start until nine for Sunday brunch customers in the morning who usually never dawdled into the café too early; but in spring now, tourists were beginning to return.

Jennifer sighed as she crept into her bedroom, trying not to disturb her mother — who slept more soundly of late — and clicked off the bedside lamp. She snuggled further under the doona, wondering if she should sacrifice sport and a social life to work seven days just because she had a goal. She worried her life lacked balance. Loneliness hit her in waves sometimes without warning and she had no idea why. Her few work friends from the office and café were all so much younger, except for Sue, who understandably spent any free time with her family.

Next morning, Jennifer found Rachel

still fully clothed and slumped across her bed, obviously having fallen asleep where she dropped. No early church service then. So she went alone, knowing her mother would make the ten o'clock family service on her own. Vicar David watched out for Rose and sometimes walked her home, using the time for tactful confidential chats.

Jennifer drew David aside at the front door after the service. 'Free for lunch today?'

'Sure.' He flashed his trademark dimpled grin.

'Great. I need to talk to you again about Rachel. And soon.'

He nodded. 'We'll work out a time.'

It occurred to Jennifer as she left the church and detoured past Grace Evans' cottage cycling to work that the dear elderly lady wouldn't be in the café any more. She would miss the petite soul who always sat so unobtrusively to one side or in a corner. Then she sighed with guilt and longing over the lovely old residence, pondering its future.

She parked her bike as always in the paved area behind the café and took the three broad steps up into the porch of the solid old double-storey red brick building that had originally been a bank. She hung up her coat and bag on the wooden clothes tree and went through into the kitchen. The warmth and aromas of coffee and cooking, plus the general buzz and clatter, hit her in a sudden and welcoming burst of life after the chill and quiet of her early morning ride.

Sue and Olivia were already at work. Sue Parker was a lively middle age with a trim figure, riotous brown curls and a passion for cooking. She unashamedly admitted that the kitchen was her heavenly domain. This one was small and efficient under its owner's sharp eye, Sue's daughter a willing worker on weekends. Her husband, John, was the only real estate agent in town running a small branch of a bigger firm in nearby Castlemaine, and they lived in the family residence upstairs. Their son, Tim, was away at university in Melbourne.

'Hi everyone,' Jennifer greeted them on her way through.

'Jen, can you put a Reserved card on table two about eleven for Keats?' Sue asked.

'Sure.' Maybe the family was taking breakfast together.

'It's just for one — their son Sam,' Sue explained, as if reading her mind.

Jennifer thought how odd to have parents in town and not be with them, especially since it seemed they had all just lost a dear friend in Grace. You'd think they would want to be together for mutual support and comfort at such a sad time.

'Right.' Jennifer paused. 'Rachel mentioned that Grace Evans died yesterday.'

'Yes.' Sue stopped what she was doing, spun around and gave Jennifer her full attention. 'It's so sad. When she was in as usual during the week, she didn't look unwell. Must have happened suddenly.'

'Be nice to think she went peacefully.'

'She was such a gentle soul, yet no one knew much about her. She was a loyal regular here. She'll be missed,' Sue said with feeling.

'Yes, she will,' Jennifer murmured. But by whom, she wondered, as she tied on her green striped apron over the standard waitress uniform of black slacks and white shirt, then moved through into the café beyond to check the Specials board.

There was the usual full breakfast fare: Devonshire teas and thick home-made soups served with traditional bush damper. Today it was vegetable. Sue was also noted for her healthy and unique combinations of fine shredded salads, plus a chunky Mediterranean version she served with pasta of the day. Her homemade rich chocolate cake was always popular and garnished with a thick dollop of fresh cream supplied daily from a local dairy. And her crêpes, legendary.

'Morning, Danni.'

Jennifer smiled at her young fellow employee, Olivia's friend, behind the counter and about to take orders from the first customers of the day within minutes of unlocking the huge wooden front door. She cruised the room, checking everything was in order. She had done her barista training and made great coffee, taking pride in her hospitality work, enjoying the variety and sociable atmosphere compared to the quieter dignified legal office where she worked behind the scenes during the week, only occasionally meeting clients.

Jennifer glanced across to where Grace usually sat and sighed, then tugged her pensive thoughts away and focused on today. She loved the cosy and historical ambience here, especially this main room with its lofty ceiling, old world charm and open fire. It had once been the customer area of the bank, except Danni now reigned behind the massive marble counter that had formerly accommodated a teller and dealt with food instead of money.

She looked out through the old-fashioned double glass doors onto the empty cobbled courtyard patio. Doubtful anyone would eat out there in this morning's chill, but the high brick walls gave shelter and Sue already had the heaters going. As the weather improved, it would become a delightful suntrap, lush with planted greenery along one side and baskets of flowers hanging from the timber beams overhead. The grapevine was still bare now but its fat serrated leaves would soon bud and unfurl to provide dappled shade all summer.

The morning grew busier as always, so when table two was eventually occupied by its reservation at eleven, Jennifer was full of interest to see the infamous Sam Keats and peeped around the espresso machine for a glimpse.

He was frowning over the menu, then looked up to view the Specials board and caught her staring. She instinctively flashed a quick pleasant smile in his direction and ducked back behind the machine to focus on the two cappuccinos and soy latte she was supposed to be making.

When the new arrival approached the counter to order from Danni at the till, she bustled past to serve the coffees, hesitating a fraction for a longer look. Easy on the eye was her first impression; older than imagined. Tall, kind of rangy and lean with a thick head of brown wavy hair. Jennifer scoffed to herself. Why did some men get all the curls? Her own hair was flat and straight. She sighed with envy as she delivered the coffees and cleared some tables on her way back.

By the time she had dumped the dirty dishes in the kitchen, the mysterious Mr. Keats had ambled back to his table with a complimentary newspaper tucked under one arm. Yes, he seemed the Sunday newspaper type, she decided.

A short time later when she reached his table bearing his order, he was staring out of the long sash window nearby, his newspaper spread out on the table in front of him but momentarily forgotten. Because it wouldn't be general knowledge yet about Grace Evans' death, Jennifer didn't say anything. Besides, she didn't know this man and didn't want to appear forward by seeming to know his private business, but she eyed him closely with compassion. He turned at her approach, a little tired around the eyes, she thought, but he probably hadn't slept well.

'Yours was the scrambled eggs, bacon and tomato?' she checked.

'No!' he snapped, scowling.

'Oh, I'm sorry.' Jennifer backed away slightly. Danni must have mixed up the orders and table numbers when she took them into the kitchen. When Mr. Keats wasn't forthcoming about his meal, she prompted, 'What was your order again, please?'

'I've given it once. I shouldn't have to repeat it,' he flared.

Jennifer was stunned by his rude blast. He wasn't to know the muddle was not her fault. But living with a lifetime of verbal lashings from her father, she no longer tolerated it from anyone. Certainly not this holier-than-thou God from the city. Fancy clothes didn't make a gentleman.

She withheld her annoyance and said, 'No, you're correct. You shouldn't. I apologise for our mistake. So to avoid it happening again,' she said with carefully pronounced patience to relay the message that she considered he had overstepped the mark of courtesy, 'I would really appreciate it if you could give me your order again and I will personally see that it's delivered correctly this time.'

Jennifer patiently bore the brunt of any dissatisfaction because she was the café front. And she had strict instructions from Sue to report each incident directly to her boss. She hesitated because Danni had only begun working behind the counter some weeks before and was Olivia's closest friend.

'It would have been quicker to make it myself at home.'

'I'm sorry you feel that way. I understand your disappointment.'

'I've a good mind to leave.'

Jennifer swallowed against her dry throat. She had learned to tactfully handle these rare hiccups and people usually understood. Not Sam Keats, it seemed.

'Please don't,' she said softly. 'My manager and chef, Sue Parker, would be horrified. She takes great pride in putting her name to this establishment.' His gaze slowly lifted to her face. Was that a note of respect in his eyes? 'Your order?' she prompted politely and braved a hesitant smile.

He sighed and she watched his shoulders droop. 'An omelette with mushrooms and bacon.'

'Thank you.' She smiled. 'I'll be back as soon as I can.'

Jennifer wasn't sure how she'd manage that. While trying to placate this one disgruntled customer, her waiting orders had backed up. In the kitchen, she personally gave Sue the order herself and stressed the situation and urgency. When she returned ten minutes later, Jennifer laid the plate of food before the esteemed Mr. Keats, still glowering and clearly unimpressed with the mistake and delay.

Jennifer sighed. There was only so much she could do. Clearly their reputation would be shattered. At least in this customer's eyes.

'I prefer my coffee after my meal,' he demanded, not looking at her.

She nodded. 'Certainly, sir. I'll make sure it's piping hot and bring it over immediately I notice you've finished your meal. Just to check, it was a long black, wasn't it?'

He paused and sent her a challenging glare. 'Yes.' Then he shook out his serviette and started eating as if she didn't exist. He and Rachel made a great pair of charmers, Jennifer thought, as she hurried back to the kitchen.

'No tips from Mr. Keats today,' she said wryly. 'He's not a happy customer,' she announced as she entered the bustling room.

Sue paused in flipping her thick, light pancakes before sliding them deftly three high onto a warm plate. 'I should go in.' She wiped her hands on her apron.

Jennifer shook her head and shrugged. 'Up to you, but I thought he was totally unreasonable. I was polite. I explained.'

Sue laid a hand on her arm. 'I know you would be, Jen, but I'm responsible for my staff.' With a shrug and a sigh, she added, 'But it was clearly Danni's error and she'll have to be told.'

'Glad it's you and not me.'

Sue chuckled. 'She wouldn't like it from you. You're her idol. Danni would be crushed if you found any fault.' Jennifer raised her eyebrows in amazement to hear such humbling flattery. 'But she'll take it from me. I often hand out discipline when she and Olivia are together. Sleepovers and the like.'

'Well, let's see how the Keats table pans out first, okay?'

Sue groaned at her howler.

Realising what she said, Jennifer chuckled, adding, 'Probably extenuating circumstances if it's because of Grace Evans' death. Clearly, she meant a lot to the family for whatever reason and they will be grieving over her loss.'

'Let it slide, you think?'

Jennifer shrugged. 'Tricky situation. Can't see it will change anything to approach him and drag out the process.'

'Sure. I'll be guided by your instincts then. I just hope he returns.'

Jennifer kept a hawk eye on table two and scooted over with Sam Keats' coffee the instant the man laid down the cutlery on his empty plate, trying not to be too obvious in her curiosity about the man who pretty much remained a mystery to everyone. He took his time over the brew and his newspaper but she was surprised to see him leave the café and fold himself into the silver compact hybrid car parked outside. Coming from his family, she had the notion he would more likely drive something sleek and black.

Jennifer managed a late short lunch break when Sue released her, but she was due back for the afternoon tea bustle that usually tapered off quickly so she might be able to leave early. When she cycled back to the flat via the scenic route into Market Lane two blocks out of her way, she grew uncomfortable over this urge to inquisitive snooping. It was unlike her. It was the cottage, she decided. The image of her mother's dream that she so desperately wanted to bring to fruition. Sam Keats' vehicle, she noted, was parked out front.

'Hope I'm not too late,' Jennifer called out as she arrived home moments later. 'Sue can only spare me for forty-five minutes.'

'We waited for you, dear.' Rose Hale pushed herself from the sofa where it looked like she had been comfortably chatting with David. Rachel slouched nearby, still in her pyjamas. 'It's all ready-served on plates and keeping warm in the oven.'

'Great. I'm starving. Hi. David.'

Jennifer blessed his kindness for keeping an eye on Rose that she knew went far beyond being his parishioner. He had an open invitation and sometimes shared Sunday lunch with the Hale womenfolk after his two morning services if he wasn't invited elsewhere.

Vicar Ormond, minus his stiff white collar and sombre black robes, looked less like any vicar anyone in the small country town had ever seen. He blew away much convention to the mixed horror yet fascination of his elderly parishioners. But the young embraced the changes and officially pronounced him *cool*. He still wore his best Sunday trousers and crisp white shirt, but a well-worn denim jacket and one gold earring publicised his untraditional personality.

In church, he encouraged modern instruments and musicians to accompany the organ, and promoted clapping to the beat. During his sermon, or Sunday chat as he called it, he ditched the pulpit and strolled down the aisle among the pews with a roving microphone as if actually speaking to people and not at them. St. Luke's Sunday services were much livelier since his arrival and attendances had increased. Word had spread.

Coupled with his curly black hair and cheeky smile, he was one hot young man and lived his ministry with such enthusiasm it was contagious. He was wholly his own person and entirely comfortable with himself in every way.

David stood and came over to greet Jennifer with an affectionate brotherly hug while Rose struggled to bring the steaming meal to the table: slices of lamb roast and gravy with roast potatoes and greens.

'Here, let me help you.' Jennifer took some of the plates and laid them on the table, glaring at her unhelpful sister. At least Rachel was out of bed.

David said grace and Jennifer eagerly tucked in, not wasting time because of her limited lunch break. In between mouthfuls, she said, 'Sam Keats came in for breakfast this morning. Alone. Boy, is he one grumpy soul.'

'He and his parents aren't close,' Rose murmured, surprising Jennifer that she knew so much. With every passing week, her vagueness about the past seemed to be slowly subsiding.

'That's a pity,' Jennifer observed. 'I wonder why? His car was parked outside Grace's cottage just now.'

'They'll have the task of clearing it all out ready for a sale I guess.' David glanced across at Jennifer and grinned with mischief. 'I guess it will be on the market soon.'

She groaned. 'Between my savings and the First Home Owners grant, I'm not sure I have enough for a deposit.'

'Give up on your stupid dream,' Rachel spluttered with her mouth full. 'It'll never happen,'

Jennifer took a moment to absorb her sister's blunt comment and not respond with words she'd later regret. 'Maybe not. But smaller properties like that are snapped up fast and I intend to be proactive about it.'

Rachel shrugged. 'You won't be the only buyer with an eye on the place.'

Perhaps to defuse a brewing argument, David said, 'Now that you mention Sam Keats being back in town, Jennifer, there's been talk around the hospital that he is on board as the architect to advise on designs for the new aged care community centre. As an honorary consultant.'

Jennifer found it hard to equate the gruff café customer with the charitable professional.

'An extremely generous gesture,' David continued, 'when you take into account loss of income and time commitment. It will save a heap of money on the overall project. Apparently it's going to be like a village with independent units, a main care premises like a nursing home with staff plus a community room for all kinds of activities and recreation facilities.'

'I can't believe the government has committed itself to dollar-for-dollar funding,' Jennifer said. 'Because of lesser population and voting power, small country areas are often neglected.'

'It's a huge boost for the area,' David agreed. 'He's to be commended on helping get it off the ground.'

Jennifer laid down her cutlery on the empty plate with a flourish. 'Mother, that was delicious. The lamb was so tender. Thanks, but,' she checked the kitchen wall clock and pushed back her chair, 'I'm out of here. Have to go.'

She grabbed her bag, planted a swift kiss on her mother's forehead, waved to Rachel and David, and left.

2

Monday morning, Jennifer was back in the office of Daltons Lawyers where she worked as Stewart Dalton's personal secretary during the week. She was keeping an eye on reception from her desk while Natalie made a cuppa in the tearoom, when Mel and Sam Keats entered through the sliding glass front doors.

Jennifer groaned as she rose from her leather swivel chair at the computer. Hopefully the son wouldn't recognise her, or their encounter would at least be civil. She ran self conscious hands down the length of her tailored straight navy skirt and tugged unnecessarily at the matching jacket.

She strode forward to greet them, smiling, glancing down quickly at Natalie's office diary to check if they had an appointment. In the back of her mind, she realised their presence might be regarding Grace Evans' estate since there didn't seem to be any family involved.

'Good morning, Mel.'

'Jennifer.' He nodded briefly, then indicated the familiar tall young man beside him. 'This is my son, Sam,' he added a mite uncomfortably, unusual for the normally blustering confident businessman. 'Sam, this is Jennifer Hale.'

Meeting a new client, she would normally have said she was pleased to meet them, but not in this case. 'We've met. Sort of. Mr. Keats,' she managed courteously, and pulled a quick official smile.

Sam's glare of recognition clung to her in challenge. Oh dear. It seemed neither of them had a good memory of the other.

She was about to pick up the phone to buzz her boss when he said, 'Jennifer,' his deep voice unusually pleasant. Then he rapped out in a completely different sharp tone, 'You were in the café yesterday?'

His assessing glare told her he definitely recalled their strained conversation. Trying for a lightness she didn't feel, Jennifer said, 'Guilty.'

'You're a busy woman,' he observed with a hint of mockery.

A criticism or a compliment? 'I love *both* my jobs,' she declared.

'Grass doesn't grow under this girl's feet,' Mel said briskly, always a smooth charmer.

Well, at least one Keats was on her side. But his comment sounded like a subtle hint of censure at Sam's expense. Jennifer watched their body language closely for a moment and sensed waves of tension crackle between the man and his son. Trouble there, she was willing to bet. Not a happy family reunion.

It became unnecessary for her to buzz her boss and announce their arrival because Stewart must have heard their voices and sauntered out from his office in his usual unhurried manner.

'Mel. Sam.' They all shook hands.

Stewart Dalton was short and trim

and had briefly retired but, after his wife died, he had returned to his profession. He kept busy but worked short days, playing social golf mid-week as well as competition on Saturdays, and thriving on people and the company. Jennifer adored her lovely boss like a favourite uncle. He was an old school gentleman who revered his post war classic black Jaguar coupé, instantly recognisable driving around town. He kept it in such meticulous condition, and always so highly polished, that Jennifer was surprised he dared risk venturing out onto the roads with his prized vehicle.

'Jennifer, dear,' he said in his soft measured voice, 'could you fetch Grace Evans' will and the title to Mr. Keats' Market Lane property from the strong room.' He pulled a polite businesslike smile, adding, 'Then perhaps a tea tray might be nice.'

'Of course,' she said as the men moved into his office while her brain buzzed with Stewart's request. She snapped on the light and entered the chill of the walk-in safe. She flipped through the will drawers and found Grace's folded document, then pulled out the batch containing Mel's many property title deeds and thumbed through until she found the right one. She stared at the front and shook her head. Mel Keats did indeed own number seven Market Lane. Grace Evans must have been a tenant all these years. The reason for the family's connection, perhaps?

Still dazed with surprise, Jennifer delivered the parchments to Stewart's office and prepared a tea tray. She hadn't needed to ask what they drank. Stewart preferred white tea with two sugars, and both Mel and Sam drank strong coffee. She knew because Mel was a regular client and she remembered Sam's order from the café yesterday morning. How could she forget such an unfortunate blunder and their resulting confrontation? Like father, like son, she reflected, adding a plate of Sue's homemade biscuits that Stewart loyally purchased from her other employer.

When Natalie returned to her desk,

Jennifer took her turn for a tea break. Back at her computer within fifteen minutes, she was disappointed to learn the Keats men had left and Stewart hovered near her desk.

'Sorry, I was just in the tea room. Have I kept you waiting?'

'Not at all,' he said generously. 'Jennifer dear, I've left some transfer papers here for you.'

At a quick glimpse, she saw the cottage property was being conveyed into Sam's name alone with no sale price.

'Any deadline?' she clarified efficiently, as she did with all work that came in. Some contracts were more urgent than others.

'No.' He smiled. 'Just place it in the queue.'

Jennifer's mind raced with an exciting possibility as he moved away, so she leapt in and asked eagerly, 'Are they going to sell it?'

'Couldn't say, my dear.' Stewart readily paused. She could ask or speak to him about anything, as much a friend as a boss.

'Is he planning to live there?'

'I have no idea. I doubt it. He's a city man after all,' Stewart replied reasonably.

Jennifer grew hugely frustrated. She must learn to be more patient. *If it's meant to be, it will happen.* She had never fully understood or appreciated the theory until now because when it came to her dream, she preferred to place her trust in reality and make it happen instead of sitting back and waiting.

'If he's not going to live here, what's he going to do with it?' She frowned. 'Not rent it out, surely?'

The wrinkles at the corners of Stewart's eyes creased more deeply as he smiled in amusement at Jennifer's interest. 'Why don't you ask him yourself?'

'I just might do that,' she said positively, not ashamed at taking the reins to forge a more secure future for her mother's sake. And knowing Stewart, he would advise her on the legalities every step of the way.

For the moment, Jennifer's visions of living in the lovely old stone cottage wavered while at the same time her mind ticked over with a sneaky possibility. She had formally met Sam Keats so, theoretically, she could tactfully approach him about his intentions. She sighed. Given their initial clash and present state of mutual caution, that didn't seem the best step to take at the moment.

But the seed had been planted and she knew it couldn't hurt to contemplate her options.

* * *

The tiny brass bell gave its familiar tinkle as Jennifer entered Mr. Wilson's secondhand shop at the far end of Main Street the following Friday, shortly before closing. She inhaled the musty air like a drug. At least once a week, a fascination for old cheap things steered her feet on the pedals and she succumbed to the urge for browsing her way among the maze of crowded aisles.

There was always the hope that the store's ancient wizened owner had acquired new stock that cried out to be rescued and promised to be salvageable for a bargain price. Most of the time she didn't know what she loved until she saw it, but at this stage, she was collecting ideas and dreaming, browsing, poring over house and garden magazines. Many she borrowed from the mobile library van that regularly visited Bundilla on its scheduled runs to small towns no longer able to sustain a bricks-and-mortar building.

For now, Jennifer indulged her aspiration, but the possibility of Grace's cottage coming up for sale was exciting and, like spring, brought forth a burst of new life in her. Easy to imagine estate agent John Parker placing a bunch of cottage keys into her eager hands.

Her favourite pieces among all the old treasures, besides shabby yet solid furniture with renovation potential, were the beautiful specimens of English china — especially Royal Albert — and jewellery. If the shop was closed, which might happen on a whim if Mr. Wilson's nose sniffed out a worthy estate sale nearby, she would peek in the window as she passed because that was where the crafty old guy enticingly displayed his new arrivals.

Mr. Wilson knew her familiar face well. In his brown scruffy checked suit with wild grey hair and sharp twinkling eyes, this afternoon he sat on the stool behind the counter.

'Afternoon, Mr. Wilson.'

'Jennifer.' He paused before continuing in his slow reedy drawl. 'Furniture auction out at the Henderson place this weekend.'

'Yes, I imagine they have some lovely things.'

She couldn't go, of course. Apart from the fact she was working and rarely managed any substantial free time — by choice, she reminded herself — the winding hills on her bike would prove a challenge and she could hardly bring anything home of a decent size. And having hauled it back to the flat, where to keep it?

Jennifer sighed. Sometimes she wondered if she shouldn't just blow her savings, buy a car and head out of town in any direction with no plan but the freedom of the open road. Instead, she had anchored herself in Bundilla, gripped by insecurity and yearning, for herself as much as her mother, in deference to a dream.

'The Evans' cottage might be on the market.'

Jennifer's radar locked onto Mr. Wilson's idle remark. What did he know that she didn't? Grace's private funeral, or so she heard, had taken place yesterday, and at Daltons the title to the property was still in the process of transfer. It was too soon for any steps to have been taken on that front, she would have thought.

'Do you know that for a fact?'

'It's rather old. Not the sort of house one would likely lease,' was his observation.

Well, if Sam Keats considered that direction, she could always apply and live in it as a rental. But that rather defeated the reason for wanting home ownership in the first place. 'I could see myself living in that cottage.' She stared vacantly past the shop wares and out the front window at nothing in particular.

'Why does a young single thing like you want to own a house?' the crusty old man muttered kindly.

'Security, Mr. Wilson,' she confessed. 'Deep down, doesn't everyone crave a tiny piece of dirt on earth that they can call their own?'

She was just mustering the motivation to force herself to leave this addictive shop of bygone things and let Mr. Wilson close up when the bell rang again, and her attention snapped to the door.

Her heart beat just that bit faster at the unexpected sight of Sam Keats. Adrenaline always kicked in when she feared something. Word was he had stayed in town all week, but Jennifer

49

hadn't seen him since Monday morning. She wondered where he'd slept and ate and kept himself hidden. Unusual in a small town like Bundilla not to see him around. Perhaps he'd locked himself away in Grace's cottage. Unless the bad blood with his parents had been settled and he stayed at Melville Park. It was not like they would be short of rooms out there.

To her annoyance, she had to admit that despite looking windblown, Sam Keats was as handsome as ever. When he caught sight of her, Jennifer managed a polite smile that he returned. All very civil — until his warm brown eyes regarded her more intently, making her immediately aware of wearing sneakers and socks with her smart office clothes for riding her bike home and realising how mismatched she must look.

He spoke first. 'Jennifer.'

She nodded. 'Sam.'

It seemed too brazen to badger him about the cottage, although she was sorely tempted because his height and proud stance suggested an aloofness that kept her wary, so she merely said, 'Lots to see in here,' as she squeezed past him on her way out.

'Just browsing?' he murmured.

She turned, halfway to the door, surprised he should open a conversation. She couldn't be on his list of favourite people. 'Always. Can't resist.'

Mr. Wilson rose from his stool and shuffled out from behind the counter. Jennifer lingered with one hand on the door, tuning her ears in their direction.

'Good morning, sir. May I help you?'

'I certainly hope so. Sam Keats,' he introduced himself and, without appearing too obvious about it, Jennifer glanced back to see them shake hands. 'I'm looking to sell some furniture and wondered if you're interested to buy.'

The bell jangled again as Jennifer left and practically skipped from the shop. Mr. Wilson would be rubbing his hands together in delight. And if Sam Keats was selling everything, surely that meant the cottage would be going up for sale?

About time she put those options into place.

* * *

Jennifer stood opposite Sue Parker's real estate agent husband, John, in his Main Street office.

'Is Grace Evans' cottage going on the market any time soon?'

John lounged against the counter, arms folded, amused. 'I haven't received any instructions to sell, Jennifer.'

'Well I'm living in hope,' she said optimistically. 'Are there any other possibilities in town at the moment?'

John smiled indulgently. 'You ask that question every few months, Jen. Answer's still the same.'

Jennifer knew she shouldn't have bothered him. Over the past year since her father's death and being crammed into the flat with her mother and Rachel, she had scoured all the For Sale photos in the local thin weekly newspaper, the Bundilla Standard. Any potential homes rarely emerged. Houses were either too big and meant for a family, or too decrepit and needed too much money and expertise to be sunk into them before becoming habitable. She had basic skills like painting but not physical tradesmen-type jobs. She was growing despondent at ever finding a place of their own. Sadly, Grace's cottage was an enticing dangling carrot that seemed unlikely to happen.

John sent her a sympathetic glance. 'You've done your homework. You know as much as me.'

'Please,' Jennifer pleaded, 'if the Evans' place comes onto the market, contact me first?'

From the outside it looked a lovely old house. She longed for a glimpse inside. Maybe she would go and peek in one of the windows.

He grinned and nodded. 'Will do.'

Despite the promise, Jennifer left John's office feeling low and discouraged. She just knew her mother would improve even further and the garden in the Market Lane cottage would make Rose's green fingers itch. Patience was this nasty little word growing in size at the back of her mind. She deflected the commonsense thinking that if she didn't achieve this acquisition for her mother, her world would not crumble.

* * *

That weekend, Jennifer was bustling among the packed tables in the café's hectic lunch rush on Saturday when the door opened and she glanced up to see Sam Keats stroll in with a mild gust of spring breeze. She caught his gaze as he tidied his ruffled hair and, as she did instinctively with all Sue's customers, she flashed him a welcoming smile. It was not returned. He looked vague and distracted, his mind clearly elsewhere.

He scoured the crowded room. With her arms full of dirty dishes and heading for the kitchen, Jennifer nodded toward the patio. He didn't acknowledge her suggestion, but emerged from his daydream enough to weave his way toward it. The glass folding doors were pushed back and the balmy mid-day sunshine drenched the sheltered space in warmth. It was a few minutes before she finished servicing three recently deserted tables and could take his order.

'Back for the weekend?' she asked, making casual conversation.

She was relieved he seemed more relaxed than other times. Being dressed in a trendy long-sleeved T-shirt pushed up to the elbows certainly helped. A chunky, flashy-looking watch gleamed at his wrist. Impossible to believe that such a smashing-looking bloke always ate alone. He never appeared with his parents or any female company. Well, at least not here in Bundilla. Melbourne would be another story, she imagined.

He merely nodded, not responding with any sign of warmth. 'I'll have the herbed Atlantic salmon and salad.'

When he folded the menu, she added, 'Can't tempt you with anything else?' The sharp questioning gaze he swung in her direction made her blush. 'I meant dessert.'

'No. Thank you for the offer. Just a long black.'

Jennifer scuttled off to the kitchen, feeling rustic and embarrassed by her unintentional gaffe. By the time his meal was ready, she had composed herself enough to face him again.

She intended just setting the plate before him, but couldn't resist asking, 'Must be lots to do at the cottage. I don't suppose it's ready to put on the market yet?'

He shook his head. 'No,' he muttered, looking uncomfortable and annoyed to be bothered.

Jennifer shrugged. 'Of course not,' she ended lamely, feeling suitably awkward. 'Enjoy your meal, then.'

The following week, Jennifer had one particularly frantic afternoon in the legal office working under pressure to prepare a pile of urgent documents ready to be signed by a client early the next morning. It was a fabulous spring day, so

Stewart had left instructions and disappeared to play golf, leaving his two assistants alone.

Jennifer had her head bent over her computer, busily keying information into a document, when Natalie put through a telephone call.

'David.' She frowned at the sound of his voice.

'Rose has collapsed while working in the vicarage garden,' he said breathlessly.

Jennifer gasped. 'Is she all right?'

'Yes,' he hastily assured her. 'The paramedics are here in the manse now and have pronounced her dehydrated. She's on a fluid drip and they're staying with her for a while. She just overdid it in the heat. They'll take her back to the flat shortly and I'll go around and stay with her until you get home.'

'Oh, David, would you? I have so much work to finish this afternoon, and Stewart never takes his mobile out onto the golf course, so I can't contact him or leave Natalie here on her own. If Rachel's home, you won't need to stay,' she offered hopefully.

'Don't worry. Your mother's recovering well. She'll just need rest.'

Jennifer sighed. 'She forgets time when she's in the garden. I bet she wasn't wearing a hat.'

David chuckled. 'No. I feel bad about not going out to check on her more often on such a warm day.'

'No one's to blame. I'll see you as soon as I can.'

Jennifer felt the added pressure to skip her tea break and work through, trying to finish her workload as soon as possible. When she eventually arrived home much later than normal, a weak Rose was asleep and David was reading the newspaper.

'Sorry I'm so late. Rachel?' she asked hopefully.

He shook his head. 'Nowhere to be seen, I'm afraid.'

After David left, having refused her invitation to stay for dinner because of a meeting, Jennifer angrily chopped vegetables while steaming rice for a stir-fry, furious that her irresponsible sister hadn't bothered to at least write a note and let them know her whereabouts. That usually remained a mystery these days. When Constable Fuller appeared at the front screen door that she had left open to admit the benefit of dusk breezes, Jennifer's instinct kicked in with a stab of alarm and a silent prayer. This was the last straw.

'Evening, Jennifer,' he greeted her.

'It's open, Richard. Come in,' she called out to the rangy young rookie cop who had swollen the local task force to two along with his immediate senior, Sergeant Davis. He was always approachable and congenial, with a mouthful of perfect teeth, often buzzing into the café to collect takeaway coffees when he was on weekend highway patrol. Tonight, Jennifer didn't like his serious expression as he walked inside and approached her.

She wiped her hands on a towel. 'It can only be about Rachel.'

He slowly nodded.

'Is she okay?'

'More or less.'

'What happened?'

'She stole some blu-ray movies and some small electronic equipment from The Emporium.'

Jennifer suffered a rush of humiliation. Mahoney's Emporium was a Bundilla icon, still trading and owned by the same family for 150 years. How could she face Jack and Laurel again? They were the friendliest people.

'As she left the store,' Richard continued while Jennifer processed the news, 'she actually stepped over the threshold of the premises and moved outside onto the footpath, so technically,' he wobbled his hand, 'it was stealing. Rachel claimed she was just looking at them to read the labels out in the light and she intended returning them to the shelf.'

Jennifer folded her arms and sighed. 'A likely story.'

'Exactly.' Richard pulled a wry grin. 'Upshot? Jack called me just to give her a scare but he doesn't intend pressing any charges against her. We've checked our records. It's her first time.'

'That we know about,' Jennifer pointed out uneasily.

'We've just given her a warning.' The constable paused. 'Actually, I've been keeping an eye on her around town lately, especially since she teamed up with Boomer Drake. In his defence, he's had a tough life.'

'Oh, Richard, thank you. Rachel hasn't been in a happy place for quite a while.'

'No. Didn't look like it,' he agreed. 'She'll work through it. Most kids do.'

'Except Rachel's not a kid anymore.'

'But she has people who care about her and that makes all the difference.'

'We don't seem to be doing much good.'

'Give her time but be firm.'

'I do and then I feel bad.' After a pause, she asked, 'Where is she now?' Jennifer rubbed her arms, imagining her little sister in the confines of a cell down at the local police station. No point bothering her mother with all this. Jennifer would just have to be more vigilant where

Rachel was concerned from now on. Her head spun with her current weight of responsibility.

Richard grinned. 'She's in my vehicle right outside, sweating a little, I hope. I told her I needed to speak to you first and she actually looked concerned. I'll go bring her in.'

'Thanks,' Jennifer said softly, moving to the door.

Richard Fuller turned from the doorway. 'I heard Rose took a turn today. She okay?'

Jennifer nodded. 'She stayed out in the sun too long. Spring's warming up. She's sleeping.'

When Rachel appeared and wandered up the driveway alone beside the flats she looked aimless and, for once, guilty. The constable waved as he drove away. Against all her better instincts, Jennifer's crap day and frustration rose to the fore the moment she closed the door.

'What were you thinking?' She didn't give her sister time to answer but added angrily, 'Crime now?'

Rachel looked shaken and unsettled as she brushed by and jammed her hands into her jeans pockets. 'Just trying to get some money.'

Jennifer scoffed. 'You're supposed to do that honestly with a decent job like everyone else. Right intentions. Wrong way of going about it.' With Rachel's back still rudely turned against her, she flared, 'Geez, Rachel, you don't remember the seventh commandment? Thou shalt not steal? Not only God's law, sis, it's common law as well.'

Rachel whirled around, eyes narrowed and glittering. 'Miss Goody Two Shoes, always spouting the Bible.'

'Laws are to live by, Rachel, for a peaceful civilised society.'

'You're so full of it!' she spat back.

Jennifer finally took a step away and a deep breath to steady her inner tension. 'Whatever,' she said more calmly. 'You should consider yourself damn fortunate Jack Mahoney isn't pressing charges.'

'Of course not. I gave the stuff back. I wasn't really going to take it.'

'You had it in your possession. You left the shop. You could have had a criminal record.' Jennifer shook her head in despair, deciding not to pursue their conversation any further. It only made her more upset and Rachel wouldn't listen anyway. She probably shouldn't have jumped on her like that but the girl had to start growing up and being accountable sometime. She would leave it for now, but there was no choice. They would need to revisit this situation.

'Dinner will be ready in fifteen minutes.'

'I'm not hungry.' A sullen Rachel pushed past and headed down the hallway.

'Don't make a noise — '

Too late. Rachel had already slammed the door. Some minutes later while Jennifer was tossing the stir-fry in the pan, her mother emerged.

'Did she wake you?'

'I was only dozing. What was that about? I heard raised voices.'

Jennifer debated telling her mother about Rachel's latest exploit, but one look at her pale face and she decided to leave it for a better time. 'A bad day.' She forced a cheery smile in her direction. 'Just you and me tonight, Mum. Feel like sharing a crisp chardonnay?' Jennifer reached into the refrigerator and held up a chilled bottle.

Rose smiled. 'Half a glass would be nice.'

As Jennifer and her mother settled down to a simple meal, she wondered what else life could throw at her, and hoped the rest of the week improved.

* * *

That same night, Sam Keats stretched out on a sofa in the rear and cosy sitting room of Grace's cottage. Beside him on the floor were two open shoeboxes he had found the previous weekend in the back of a bedroom wardrobe. The contents had stunned him: bundles of letters written by Grace's fiancé, Peter Charlton, while stationed in Vietnam during the war. It had been a jolt to actually see Peter's handwriting, making the man more real to him, bringing him alive although he had been gone for over thirty years.

Sam became so engrossed in reading, treasuring every word, that he made the decision to stay in Bundilla for the week. A quick phone call to his business partner late Sunday night advised him of the change of plans. They hastily discussed their current design commissions and construction projects, working out how to reorganise and shuffle their work-loads so no clients were disadvantaged until Sam's return the following week.

Meanwhile, Sam had sprinted down to Bundilla's one and only grocery store minutes before it closed to stock up on basics for his extended stay. Since then he had virtually lived like a hermit in the cottage, parking his car out back in the orchard to reduce his visibility and be left alone to sink himself into another world and time.

He was slowly coping with the bombshell Mel and Barbara had delivered on the night Grace died. Strangely, the letters helped his acceptance of their revelation. Sam folded up the letter he had just read, tucked it back into its envelope and pulled out the next.

Nui Dat
My dearest heart,
Here I am in a strange place halfway around the world, making it through one day at a time. I'm sitting here in the mud and heat, with wet feet all the time, and infections. It is hot and dirty. I don't feel like eating and crave anything cold.

I live in a tent with other blokes and am looking at your beautiful photograph. It is like you are from another world. I want to be with you. I miss you more than anything and think it is so unfair to be so happy and engaged to you, then be torn apart.

There was more but it ended: *Yours forever, Peter.*

They were all written along similar lines. He read others until he unfolded one that began, as always, from Nui Dat with *My dearest heart.*

I have only spent a few months in Vietnam, but like most blokes over here it feels like an eternity since we parted in Sydney. Life for me is all about survival, loneliness and hope.

Charlie [the Vietcong] controls most of the country. The villagers know the situation but are friendly and unconcerned. Whenever we go out on road sweep patrols checking for mines and the enemy, we do lots of walking. We get to see the Vietnamese and how they live. Everyone is so poor. They all farm but there are no tractors. They plough with water buffalo and work the paddies by hand. Buildings are shacks.

I showered in the rain yesterday. Can you believe there is a shortage of water? My life is in this country for now but I am not all here. You know I left part of me behind with you: my heart and my love. The days of the week make no difference. I just live for the future with you and better days.

Yours forever, Peter.

As Sam came to the last of the carefully stored letters in the box, he opened it with mixed feelings. Again, Nui Dat, and again, *My dearest heart.*

I have hesitated to tell you the truth, but you are a nurse; I need to share with you and for you to know what it is really like over here. There is the constant sound of artillery and we leap into the trenches if we are not out on patrol. A rocket missed me two days ago but hit mates nearby. We were on a steamy rubber plantation waiting for the VC.

War is so random and impersonal. I find myself filled with anger. Good men being killed or wounded in a rotten useless war. When is any conflict justified? My hope is always only to survive Vietnam and build my life

*with you when I get back to Australia.
I live for the day when I can hold you
again. Thoughts of you give me something to live for. You know that I love
you very much.*

Yours forever, Peter.

*PS — we just got word to move
out. We're always on patrol. Going
someplace and back again.*

Judging by the dates, this must have
been the last letter Peter wrote to Grace
before he was killed. Sam could only
presume that the patrol had been his
final fateful mission. He cursed at the
gut-wrenching injustice that took Peter's
life and split the heart and dreams of
the young woman left behind. Grace.

Sam frowned and shook his head in
denial that such a deep love at any time
— but especially during war — was
risky, and exposed a person to such
sorrow and tragedy. He wasn't sure he
could open his heart so much to another.
After his recent discovery, he decided
he had been hurt enough and would

70

focus on his work. All the same, he admired Peter Charlton for being man enough to declare his heart to a woman and lay it bare.

When Sam finished Peter's letters, he started on Grace's diaries, a precious and irreplaceable cache of her life. To his benefit, and judging by the hoarded contents of the cottage, Grace had thrown nothing away of value.

It was only as he flipped through more and more pages over the years for the corresponding dates to Peter's letters from Vietnam, to see what she had written during that time to compare, that the puzzle pieces began slotting together. A deeper truth and unsettling breach of trust and broken promise emerged. The shock of this new disclosure changed to a rising anger in him.

Not only did her words and sentiments express her true love for Peter, and grief when denied a life together through the tragedy of war, but as the years passed, it eventuated that Grace had been deprived of the only other special light in her life.

Sam's heart ached as he scanned the lines.

I feel so sad and betrayed because 'my Samuel' has been sent away. And only ten. I will rarely see him. I have nothing of you now, Peter. They have taken away my joy in living.

With a resentful heart, Sam now realised how much he meant to Grace, because each time he made a reluctant or grudging visit to his *Aunt* as he knew her, he now understood that the sparkle in her eyes had not only been the humour of her personality that always shone through, but her happiness at seeing her son.

And from looking at the precious photos of Peter Charlton, his father, they were so alike. It must have been bittersweet for Grace to see him and have her thoughts drawn back to Peter and what she lost. Bad enough to be robbed of a fiancé, but to be also cheated of her son was outrageous and unforgiveable.

As Sam's indignation mounted, so did his impatience and need to tackle those responsible: of all people, Mel and Barbara — whom Grace had trusted to keep their word. He kept reading until he was sure he had all the facts as Grace had recorded them, then bundled the two relevant diaries under his arm and strode for his car.

He was speeding down sleepy Main Street, brimming with outrage, his mind elsewhere, heading for the other end of town and the road out to Melville Park, when a bicycle loomed out in front of him and he slammed his foot on the brakes.

3

Jennifer screamed in fright as the vehicle wandered onto her side of the street. She wobbled to avoid it but it clipped her handlebars and she lost her balance, spinning around and feeling herself thrown onto the unforgiving asphalt.

Bruised, grazed and terrified, she lay still a moment, blinking hard and looking up at the sky to gather her wits over what had just happened. Fortunately, she was wearing long sleeves and slacks — now bloodstained and ripped, she noticed, groaning as she tried to sit up. At least her clothes appeared to have protected her bare skin against worse injuries.

Then a white-faced Sam Keats appeared over her and knelt down. 'God in heaven, Jennifer, are you all right?'

'This is Australia. We drive on the

left-hand side,' she blasted in shock, wincing in pain as he helped her struggle to her feet from under a battered heap of bicycle. Her shaking hands fumbled with the chinstrap of her helmet.

Sam frowned. In his rage and poor concentration, had he actually strayed onto the other side of the road? His thoughts had been focused on the strips he planned to tear off Mel and Barbara.

Jennifer had no pity for him. He *should* look gutted.

'My fault entirely. I'm so sorry.' He pushed a distressed hand through his thick wavy hair.

'Where on earth were you going in such a hurry?' she muttered, dusting herself off, stretching her limbs, making sure everything still worked. 'It's only five minutes to anywhere in Bundilla. You're never going to be late.'

Chastised, he said humbly, 'Come and sit down for a moment,' as he righted her twisted bicycle with one hand and drew her toward a small nearby park with the other.

'I can manage Treadly.' She grabbed the handlebars. 'You should move your car from the middle of the street.'

He did as he was told. As Sam climbed back in and parked, Jennifer hobbled over to the bench seat in the park and gratefully sank down, starting to tremble and feeling ill.

When Sam joined her, he asked anxiously, 'Are you sure there's nothing broken? Perhaps we should call 000?'

Jennifer vigorously shook her head. 'Absolutely not. I'll be fine, I'm sure. Just shaken.'

This new side of Sam Keats surprised and charmed her. No glimpse of his guarded side today, so she was forced to consider him in a kinder light.

He spared her poor mangled bicycle a rueful glance. 'I'll take it down to the garage and get it fixed.'

'George will be closed by now.'

'I'll see what I can do.' His confidence conveyed the impression he could open doors and work minor miracles. Jennifer hoped this was one of them. Treadly was her only transport. Looked like she might be walking for a day or two.

'Meanwhile I'll run you home.'

'But you were clearly on your way to somewhere else.'

Sam glanced at her in startled surprise, as though the accident had blitzed whatever else had been on his mind. She knew the feeling.

'It can wait.' He sounded disappointed.

Jennifer refused to feel bad about his delay, since he had caused the accident. In the light of a more mellow Sam and a respite from their usual verbal sparring, she was just starting to believe the day, despite the mishap, might be looking up, when his mother's familiar BMW coupé slid smoothly to the kerb across the street. The car was always identifiable around town for the flashy statement and person it represented.

Barbara Keats stepped out, perfectly groomed as always, dressed in tailored slacks, a stylish top and her trademark pearls. She crossed to them in determined strides, the usual superior expression on her face.

Jennifer heard Sam's low curse and she darted a questioning glance at him. He looked as though he has seen a ghost.

With a tight face, he muttered, 'Don't ask.'

'Sam.' Barbara pulled a stiff smile. 'Jennifer,' she acknowledged, disapproval clear on her face as though she should dare keep company with her son. 'Shouldn't you be in the café?'

Jennifer shut her mouth against snapping out a smart rejoinder. 'I'm on a break.' She had been dashing home quickly to check on her mother until she was abruptly stopped.

Barbara turned an ignorant shoulder to Jennifer and addressed her son. 'Mel thinks we should talk.'

Jennifer watched Sam's thunderous face and straightened in amazement at his fierce response. 'We most certainly do. I was on my way.'

So that's where he'd been going. But why the rush?

'What stopped you?'

'He ran into me,' Jennifer quipped, feeling far from chirpy but wanting to explain, then realising what she had said. She was rewarded by her first mischievous returning grin from Sam. What an attractive change it made to his whole face.

'You can ride with me,' Barbara suggested, moving away, obviously expecting Sam to follow.

'I have my own car,' he snapped.

'You can come back for it later.'

'No. I'll be out shortly.'

Haughty at his lack of cooperation, and probably unaccustomed to having her demands ignored, Barbara pouted, 'Well, don't be long. It's getting late. Unless you're staying for dinner.'

'I haven't been invited.'

By now, Jennifer was gaping in astonishment at this crisp exchange. No love lost here. What an eye-opening scandal. Barbara Keats' treatment of her son was appalling. As she treated everyone else. With condescension. From the grim determination on Sam's face, she could see he was restraining his temper and trying to stay polite.

Well done, she thought, smiling at him in encouragement. He pulled a wry grin and the first sparks of alliance flared into life between them. Jennifer filled with a warm glow. Any wonder Sam never returned to Bundilla? How unfortunate to have Barbara Keats as your mother.

Sam sat rigidly beside her, making no attempt to move, sending a clear signal to the other woman that she was dismissed.

With a careless shrug of her shoulder, Barbara turned on her smart heels and strode back to her gleaming luxury car. The tyres screeched as she sped away.

Heaving a deep sigh, Sam placed a hand at Jennifer's elbow and said, 'Shall we go?'

In silence, she allowed herself to be settled into his comfortable car. They didn't speak on the short ride home, for Sam's simmering fury meant he was not in any mood for idle conversation, and she was clenching her teeth against her aches and pains.

As he opened the car door for her back at the flat, he said, 'I'll tell George your bicycle repair is urgent and have him call you when it's done.'

'That's very thoughtful. Thank you.'

'How will you get back to the café?'

'After attending to my wounds and a cuppa, I'll be fine. I can walk back slowly.'

'Want me to come back in, say, thirty minutes?'

'Your parents are expecting you.' Did she imagine a wince? 'I wouldn't want to — '

'They can wait.'

'No, really, it's all right. It's barely a ten-minute walk.'

Sam looked hesitant to leave. That in itself raised Jennifer's spirits, but perhaps it had more to do with his reluctance to keep his impending appointment. 'If you need anything as a result of our collision, please let me know.'

It was only after he drove away that Jennifer realised he hadn't offered his mobile number. She supposed she could drop into Grace's cottage. A great excuse. Funny how everyone, herself included, still referred to it that way. They should be calling it Sam's cottage now, but somehow it didn't quite have the same ring.

* * *

'Why do I attract all the snapping turtles of the world?' Jennifer moaned as she backed through the kitchen swing door in the café later with an armful of empty plates, still reeling from her uncomfortable encounter with Sam's mother but also because she caught her bruised hip. She'd be black and blue all over for weeks. Sam was at fault but she held no resentment. It could have been worse and she was thankful she'd escaped with limited injuries. Not her business, of course, but she wondered what Sam had to discuss with his parents that sounded so desperate.

She left the crockery in the sink for Olivia to rinse and stack into the dishwasher.

Sue looked up. 'Rachel?'

The chef was searing an eye fillet streak to medium rare and the aroma of meaty charring made Jennifer's hungry stomach grumble. Shaken up after the accident, she'd had no appetite for lunch except a huge mug of tea while she smeared liniment onto her tender limbs where the bruises were sure to follow. She'd gone home to check on her mother, who ended up playing nurse to her daughter instead. How the tables were turned, she mused.

'Yes,' she admitted, 'But Barbara Keats, too. What on earth have I ever done to her except go out of my way to be polite? Honestly, some people think they're a gift to humanity. We're all born onto this earth and leave it the same way.' Jennifer rarely fired up, but she was on a roll today. 'Some people just don't get that what we do with the middle bit is so precious. Would it hurt those types of people to be civil?'

Sue shook her head and grinned, sliding the cooked steak onto a plate. 'Don't beat yourself up. Ignore her.'

Jennifer shrugged. 'Lady Keats, I can. Rachel, I can't.'

Sue paused as she garnished the steak. 'She's twenty-one, Jen. I know your mother's still unwell and you feel responsible, but there comes a time when you have to let them go and make their own mistakes.'

'Great advice,' Jennifer admitted. 'In theory. I don't want to bother Mum and jeopardise her recovery. She's doing so well. As the oldest and the only other family here, I'm prepared to do that for her a while longer.'

'Fair enough,' Sue shrugged. 'But, seriously? Think about it.' She glanced across at her daughter, flushed from the heat of steam from the open dishwasher and listening in on the conversation. 'Tough love works, I can assure you.'

Olivia grinned. 'We have our moments, but at least I know Mum's strict with discipline sometimes because she cares.'

Food for thought, Jennifer had to agree — but rather more difficult to put into practice.

* * *

Sam supposed he should consider it timely running into Jennifer Hale. He grimaced at the pun, but the encounter made him feel sick and grateful that she had only been frightened and bruised. Thank God the bike had taken the worst of it. Still, the clash had given him time to cool down and collect his thoughts.

As he drove between the impressive stone pillars of Melville Park, past the personalised wrought iron gates, he knew what he intended to say.

The oak trees that lined the long gravelled driveway leading to the homestead had been saplings in his childhood and still immature during the holidays of his adolescence. In the fifteen years since, spanning university and a successful architectural career, they formed a mature and shaded leafy arch overhead. He hadn't been here in years.

As the sprawling limestone house emerged into view, Sam shook his head. Far too big for two people, and it had even been extended, he noticed. But Mel and Barbara were renowned socialites. Many parties spilled from the opulent rooms and out onto the immaculate lawns. Drinks were taken on the patio or by the heated pool and its manicured surroundings. A tennis court sat idle further out. All designed for Mel to entertain and manoeuvre big company bosses who held lucrative monopolies in the construction industry.

Sam swung his car around and pulled up beneath the porte cochère. He retrieved Grace's diaries from the passenger seat beside him and took the broad steps to the impressive double front doors two at a time. When he pressed the bell, it echoed through the house. He could have parked around the back and entered by the informal rear entrance but, filled with defiance, he decided to see how they received him.

He heard approaching footsteps and was greeted by an unsmiling efficient maid. 'This way please.' She ushered him toward the formal front sitting room with its deep plush cream leather sofas and thick woollen floor rugs cushioning the gleaming floor tiles beneath.

'It's all right.' Sam smiled comfortably at the surprised maid and deliberately changed course, indicating the direction of low voices. 'I'll find them myself.'

'Yes, sir.' The maid looked confused but politely disappeared.

He hoped the element of surprise unsettled them. They were drinking red wine in the huge sparkling black and white kitchen, furiously talking in a lively exchange. Tall and imposing, casually handsome in jeans, an open-necked shirt and sports jacket, Sam was amused to see two pairs of eyes snap in his direction at his unexpected approach.

'Son!' Mel covered his shock, set down his glass and stepped forward with an outstretched hand and a smile.

Sam shook it.

Barbara's welcome was frosty. 'You took your time.' She stood her ground, leaning against the counter. Sam knew he was expected to go to her for the obligatory air kiss on each cheek but, instead, he sank one hand into his trouser pocket, with the diaries tucked under his other arm, and merely nodded in her direction.

'Barbara.'

She took a large sip of her wine and started to leave the room. 'We'll be more comfortable in the sitting room.'

'Here's just fine.' Sam dropped the diaries onto the counter with a thud.

Barbara halted mid-stride, startled by his action, and hovered uncertainly, more accustomed to being obeyed than commanded.

'I don't suppose I could have one of

those?' Sam dipped his glance at the open wine bottle on the counter. Might help steady the nerves that had kicked in since his arrival. This whole place was daunting and brought back lonely memories.

'Of course, my boy.' Mel splashed the ruby liquid into another glass and handed it to him.

Sam took a long swallow and settled on a stool around the other side so he faced them both. Essential for what he had to say. He needed to watch their expressions. Barbara stepped uncertainly closer and refilled her glass.

'We're pleased to have you back,' Mel said, smooth and charming as always, probably believing there was nothing wrong and assuming they were welcoming Sam back into their fold. 'You've had a lot to process.'

'The reason I stayed away wasn't because you should have told me twenty years ago while Grace was still alive. I've been busy reading Peter's letters from Vietnam that she kept.' He tapped the diaries. 'And these have proved most revealing.'

Mel shuffled uncomfortably, his hard stare telling Sam he was already in defensive business mode. 'In what way?'

'According to Grace — and I have no reason to disbelieve such a gentle lady — you broke a promise to her.'

'I don't know what you're implying, son — '

'You can stop calling me that right now. You adopted me and took me in but until you recover my respect, you have no right to use that word.' His gaze encompassed Barbara, wide-eyed and silent. 'I appreciate you both raised me with wealth and every educational advantage, but what I've learned this past week just proves to me what kind of people you really are.'

'Now hold on a minute, Sam. When we adopted you, Grace swore us to secrecy that you were her son. She didn't want you told.'

'I know. That's not my issue. You promised my mother you would raise and school me here in Bundilla so she could watch me grow up. What's your explanation for breaking your word and sending me away when I was ten?'

'We wanted you to have the best,' Mel protested.

'You lied to my mother and broke her heart.' He pushed the diaries toward them. 'Read her words for yourself. I've made it easy and marked the pages so I don't waste your valuable time. I realise you have no scruples about bulldozing people in business, but to deliberately cheat a powerless woman, using a child as an excuse, and claim to be doing it for my own good, is disgraceful.'

The truth hit home as Barbara stared, speechless, and Mel clamoured for excuses. 'You have the situation all wrong, Sam.'

'Not according to my mother,' he flung back. 'You didn't even have the decency to ask her first. Talk it over. Find out what she thought. You deliberately deprived a mother of her son and separated us.'

'You were just a kid then, Sam. You

didn't know any difference.'

'Read it!' He glared at Barbara. 'I can't believe you ever had the nerve to call yourself Grace's friend when you treated her like that. I was all she had in her life after Peter was killed. Her only link and memory to the man she loved and lost. My father. What you did to my mother was the lowest form of emotional abuse.'

'I'm sure Grace understood that we sent you away so you could have every advantage in life,' Mel reasoned lamely.

'Bullshit! I bet you never asked her.' Silence. 'I thought so.' He picked up one of the diaries and shook it in Mel's face. 'She bled with every word she wrote on the page. She was totally at your mercy. Yes, I get that you formally adopted me and that gave you certain legal rights, but what about your moral rights, too? And a promise? She trusted you and believed you would keep your word.'

A white-faced Barbara emptied another glass of wine and poured another while a confounded Mel, for once, had nothing to say.

Exhausted from the confrontation, Sam said, 'You're always boasting about your good word in business, Mel. Seems it doesn't matter in your personal life. The pair of you are nothing more than heartless human beings. Ambitious social climbing snobs. Grace and Peter were better people than you'll ever be. You gave me no sense of family or love. I was just the nuisance male heir to be unloaded to private school as soon as possible. I have to wonder why you bothered to adopt me in the first place.'

'Barbara can't have children,' Mel said quietly, looking across at his wife.

Sam stopped in shock as he absorbed that sad piece of news. He hadn't known. For the first time in his life, Barbara showed genuine emotion. Usually cool and composed — some would say hard — her stricken face almost crumbled, but her poise ruled and the glistening tears in her eyes did not escape.

'Then I'm sorry.' He wasn't totally heartless and sympathised with her helplessness. 'But you bungled your one chance to fully embrace what I imagine is one of life's most rewarding opportunities. To raise a child. And you stripped my mother of any right and hope she had to participate in mine.' Sam looked from one to the other, standing humiliated and dumbfounded by his outburst. 'I wonder if either of you realise the depth of what you did.' He glared at them. 'No excuse can ever justify your betrayal.'

Sam drank the last of his wine and rose from the stool. 'I hope you can be bothered to read my mother's diaries. If you do and your hearts are moved in even the smallest way, I suggest you go out to her grave, get down on your knees and beg her forgiveness.'

As he strode for the door, Sam delivered a parting shot. 'After learning more about them, I can only say I am proud and honoured that Grace Evans and Peter Charlton are my parents.'

The truth of Sam's words finally affected Barbara, who lurched against the counter, her lips trembling. Mel moved to her side, an arm about her shoulder, scowling, back straight with pride but no sign of remorse or apology.

Sam's legs felt weak beneath him as he marched from the homestead. He had taken no pleasure in the confrontation, but it was a duty he felt obliged to carry out on behalf of Grace and Peter. He had to sit behind the wheel of his car for a moment to take stock and compose himself before he could drive back into town to retreat to the cottage and lick his emotional wounds.

He was not without regrets himself that the Keats part of his life seemed to be over, at least for now. His boyhood years had been lonely, unloved, but filled with adventure on this estate. Easy to escape to its hidden corners for hours when his father was on the phone or at his construction office. And Barbara? At the hair salon, beauty clinic, or away for days shopping in Melbourne. Had her life been so empty? Even with the blessing of a child she couldn't produce herself? Had she really wanted Sam, or had she succumbed to Mel's pressure? His unspoken plan had always been for the adopted son to be his successor in the business. Never on the cards. Sam's imagination and love of nature springing from his ramblings on the estate grounds meant he ultimately preferred designing buildings, not constructing them. In particular, homes. For happy families.

Now — he sighed — the next chapter was beginning. He must adjust to this new situation of reluctant and imperfect adoptive parents, grasping at an opportunity but misusing it, against the knowledge now of what appeared to be two warm and wonderful people, his natural parents, who revealed themselves so openly in letters and diaries. He would never undervalue Mel and Barbara's role in his life. They had done their best. But he mourned the lack of Peter and Grace.

Who knew what the future held for him? He silently blessed his natural parents for their simple honesty and leaving him, even beyond death, with a precious legacy of themselves in words and deeds.

★ ★ ★

Why Jennifer tortured herself in a hopeless situation she couldn't explain, but it had become her habit to ride past Grace's cottage on her way to work to or from either the office or café. This Saturday morning, she was early and noticed the front door tantalisingly ajar with Sam's car parked on the street. It had been missing all week but he must be back for the weekend. On impulse, and because she felt more comfortable now to make an approach, she jammed on her bike brakes and leant Treadly — now perfectly restored to health — against the flaking white paint of the front picket fence. The opportunity was too tempting to resist.

She wound her way along the brick paved garden path overhung with massed greenery and pockets of natura-lised bulbs all popping up their buds and opening blooms everywhere. Even this early in the day before the sun warmed and drew out their fragrances, scents floated in the air about her. On reaching the porch, she gently prodded the door open wider with a forefinger and poked her head inside.

'Hellooo?' When there was no answer, she called out louder, 'Anyone here?'

Silence. Sam must be somewhere around. Jennifer boldly took a few steps inside to sneak a glance into the rooms on either side of the long wide carpeted hallway, slowly edging her way toward the rear.

The Victorian origins were evident in the carved plaster arches and mould-ings, generous fireplaces, ceiling rosettes, large rooms and solid furniture. It looked a bit crammed, she thought, but appeared to be in a reasonable condition consider-ing its age, and structurally sound. Mostly. She spied the occasional fine-feathered crack in a wall here and there but ignored them. Nothing disastrous, she decided, if the house was still standing after more than a century. But then the romanticism of this cottage had rather nuzzled its way into her psyche so she was inclined to put the best spin on everything about it. Lots of serious cleaning and coats of paint would give it a huge boost in appearance, removing its neglected air.

It did surprise her in one room, though, to see the bed dismantled, its frame propped against the wall and a made-up mattress on the floor. Sam must be sleeping here, preferring to be on site to sort everything out. Or, the Keats family disharmony went deeper than people knew.

At the end of the hall, yet another panelled wooden door stood ajar, and she could hear scuffling from the other side. Moving towards it, she cleared her throat and made some noise to warn of her approach.

As she pushed the door fully open, it was to see Sam crouched down shuffling through the papers and contents of what looked like a sturdy archival box. For the moment, her attention framed him in the bigger picture with the first teasing rays of morning sunlight filtering across the slate floor through French windows along the back wall behind him. She stood breathless, utterly captivated by the pretty view that overlooked an equally rambling rear cottage garden, as wild and green and colourful as out the front. The whole room was wide and vast — a combined kitchen, dining and living area.

Perhaps from some slight movement or sound she made as she entered, Sam suddenly became aware of her presence. His tousled bent head shot up and he stared at her. He jolted to his feet, as though his mind has been totally absorbed, caught up in another world of whatever it was he was doing, and her appearance brought him back.

'Good morning. Sorry to disturb you.' She smiled and gestured behind her. 'The door was open and I called out but no one answered.'

Caught off guard, he hastily stuffed all the papers back into the box as though guilty, and replaced the lid. His jeans and long-sleeved T-shirt were flecked with dust and bits of paper as though he had been rummaging for hours already. So casually dressed, he looked helpless and appealing. The image somehow made him more approachable, which perfectly suited the reason for her visit.

'Jennifer!' He looked totally surprised by her sudden appearance, but not displeased, she hoped.

'Did you eventually make that meeting with your parents last weekend?'

Sam turned pale. 'More or less. All healed?' he asked, swiftly changing the subject.

'My scratches all have scabs and my bruises have turned yellow.' She smiled. 'So I guess that's a yes.'

There was an awkward pause before he asked, 'Can I help you?'

'I know this is an awful intrusion, but when I saw your car out the front and the front door open . . . I do respect your grief in sorting through all this — '

'Do you?'

His unexpected bluntness confused her. The nice man had gone and the grump was back. Honestly, she thought women were supposed to be the moody ones.

'Er, yes,' she stammered, caught off guard by his sharp retort, and she clasped her hands together tight. 'Actually I do,' she said softly. 'I lost my father last year and it's not easy sifting through the personal things of someone close.'

His hard glare of challenge softened as though in the light of her explanation he realised how cold and abrupt he must have sounded. 'I'm sorry. I didn't know.'

'Well, you wouldn't. You don't live here. Unless your parents told you.'

There was that sharp flash of pain across his face again. 'No, they didn't.' He hesitated. 'I don't get back to Bundilla, I'm afraid.'

Make that never. Until Grace Evans'

death, neither Jennifer nor anyone else had ever seen him. 'No need to explain. That's your business, not mine.' She could have bit her tongue at her sharpness. Words usually flowed a little more politely from her mouth. 'Are you all right?' He looked like a small lost boy. Amid all this confusion — she glanced around them — was there any wonder?

'Of course,' he said bluntly.

Something niggled her about his mood. It was like one day he had it under control, the next he didn't. She decided to move on. 'I understand you're back for the proposed aged care residence complex, too?'

'Yes. Doing my bit for the community.'

Admirable when he didn't live here.

'Not much funding floating about anywhere at the best of times, but even less for small towns and populations,' he went on more easily now. 'I'm advising with the design, so it's eco-friendly and based on passive solar principles. It should help with lower running costs long term.'

While he rambled on, enthused with his subject, Jennifer noticed the light of excitement in those big brown eyes that enticed a person into their depths and transferred his passion to his audience.

'Sounds sensible in these times of global warming and concern for the environment.'

When another embarrassing silence fell between them, she took the chance to quickly glance about. She was due at work and she might never see this place again. Sam had clearly begun the process of sorting and dismantling a lifetime's collection. The dining table remained, but the living room felt sparse, as though furniture had already been moved. Some empty and partly filled boxes were scattered around; cupboard doors hung open in the compact kitchen with its cream and black Esse cooker that perfectly fitted into the country style.

'I've never been inside this house before.'

'Few people have.'

'No, I guess not. Miss Evans was a private person.'

'With good reason.' There was a defensive note in his reply.

Jennifer wondered what it was. She hesitated before deciding to press on with her mission. She had nothing to lose, but she must watch the clock. Time was running short for making it to the café by nine.

'If you're clearing everything out, I gather you don't intend to live here yourself?'

'No.'

'Would you be leasing it?'

'No.'

She had no right to know his plans, of course, which was possibly why he was not forthcoming. She wondered if his cool attitude was his normal manner. But then why shouldn't he be? She was a complete stranger bounding into his personal space when he probably preferred to be left alone, especially after just losing a dear old family friend. She remembered her own grief when her father died, even though he had been a hard soul, and realised she should be more sympathetic. Maybe he was annoyed at her rude invasion of his privacy, or at being interrupted in the middle of cleaning out an entire old house that must have much of Miss Evans' lifetime of accumulation in every cupboard. Especially if he was only in Bundilla for a short while. She gnawed her lip and felt a twinge of regret that she had so selfishly and hastily marched into the house.

'Actually, that's why I stopped. If you're not going to live here yourself or rent it out, I don't suppose it will be up for sale in the near future?'

'Definitely not.'

'Oh.' His objection was so severe, Jennifer swallowed and took a moment to collect her composure enough to hide her raging disappointment, especially after Mr. Wilson had raised her hopes with the prediction that Sam would sell. 'Not ever?' she gingerly probed, seeing her raised expectations dissolve.

He pushed out an impatient sigh. 'Not for the moment, no.'

Jennifer felt her forehead wrinkle into a frown of possibility. Not utterly hopeless then. Her dashed feelings and lingering hope of a dream becoming reality had begun slipping away, but he had said *Not for the moment*. Surely that meant there was some likelihood in the future?

She found herself being confidentially honest, but he was looking at her with those big brown eyes and saying little, so that she couldn't stop herself blathering on.

'Well, if you ever decide to rent or lease or sell it, I would really like you to give me first option on all counts.'

He stared at her long and hard, and Jennifer thought he would tell her to mind her own business and find the door. Then his mouth tilted up ever so slightly in amusement — a rare glimpse of another possible side to this man. 'Would you? Rather presumptuous.'

'Probably.' She shrugged. 'Nothing

ventured. I don't normally push into people's front doors and beg . . . ' She felt awkward now, and embarrassed by her silly gushing outburst, but remained determined to state her case. 'But I would really appreciate you giving serious thought to what I've asked. If the time ever comes, of course.'

'Don't hold your breath.' It wasn't a warning; more like a prediction. 'It won't be any time soon.'

'Fair enough. Just so you know.' She managed a pinched smile.

Sam bent to heave a huge cardboard storage box into his arms and stepped forward, as if giving her the hint to leave. She noticed another box on the kitchen bench.

'Can I help?' Jennifer moved towards it.

'No!' he snapped. Then perhaps realising how abrupt he sounded, he said more gently, 'Still sorting through that one.'

His rejection was defensive, even a little secretive, as though he didn't want her to see the contents. And in his wild objection when he had swung around toward her in warning, the box in his arms had tilted and the lid dislodged, allowing papers and photographs to slide down onto the floor.

Jennifer obligingly stooped to pick them up. She stared at one photograph for a moment, trying to identify the subject, until she recognised a much younger Grace Evans.

'She was quite lovely,' Jennifer said casually as she replaced the picture back on top of the other contents. 'I only knew her when she was older, of course, in recent years since I've lived in town.'

When she glanced across at Sam, his face was blank and sad. He had shut down again, making her aware he preferred to keep his distance, for whatever reason. Still, when he stared at her for long moments, probably against his will she reasoned, she wriggled self-consciously. He had this intense way of gaping at people. Most unsettling. And yet he couldn't seem to help himself. An edge of interest glittered in his warm gaze, as though he was making a study of thirty-year-old women from small towns. Or she was some kind of rare specimen that snagged his fascination.

Jennifer wondered how he landed the task of clearing out the cottage when she presumed his mother might at least be here working alongside to help. But of course, as rumour had it, they didn't get on. There must be a lifetime of stuff buried away behind cupboard doors.

'How long will you be in town?' Jennifer asked, moving ahead of him toward the door and opening it wider to let him pass.

'Weekends until this is all sorted.' He sounded resigned. 'For the next month or so I imagine.'

'I daresay it's a daunting task.' To ease the tension in the air between them, she found the courage to add, 'I was surprised to learn after your visit to the office with your father the other day that Miss Evans didn't own this cottage.' She smiled faintly when he didn't respond. 'I guess having lived here for so long, everyone assumed she did.'

'Natural conclusion,' he muttered.

'She had no family?' Jennifer probed, as they moved awkwardly around each other and out onto the porch.

He glanced back over his shoulder and scowled. 'Her early life was unfortunate. A lost love.'

'Oh.' Jennifer was moved to compassion by the image of a young woman's life wasted. She wondered what had happened. Whatever the circumstances, Grace had apparently never recovered nor married.

At the gate before parting, she said, 'Good luck with all your sorting. And please keep me in mind when you make any decisions.' She cringed against his possible reaction but felt compelled to put in a word anyway. He only nodded and headed for his car. At least she had taken the opportunity to plant the suggestion in his mind. And it wouldn't hurt to investigate her finances. Just in case. Strange man, though, Jennifer thought as she cycled away. Not big on conversation. Hard to get to know. Just when you thought you had him figured, his personality changed again. He let you catch glimpses of a lighter side, even let a rare grin escape. Cautious in his friendships? Everyone was a product of their childhood. She suspected the enigmatic Sam Keats was afraid to let himself be happy.

* * *

To her relief and delight, Stewart Dalton was able to help Jennifer confirm her eligibility for the First Home Owners grant that amounted to some thousands of dollars. Added to her savings, it would make a healthy deposit, placing her in a sound position to buy the cottage. Should the chance arise.

She sighed. Now she only had to wait and hope. Few other likely properties ever came onto the market in Bundilla.

Grace Evans' cottage had captured her interest. The dear old soul was such a mystery. So many questions remained unanswered.

4

The last person Jennifer expected to see waiting for her as she left the café a week later was Sam Keats, who was leaning against the bonnet of his car, arms folded, looking dreamy but unsure. He ventured a sheepish smile and, as always, it completely changed him from moody to gorgeous. Like a cloud had been lifted from his soul.

Her heart surged with warmth and something shifted into place between them. Was he here to ask her on a date?

'Don't worry, it's parked,' he quipped, indicating his car. 'You're safe.'

'Such a relief.' She laughed at his humour and friendliness. Now she felt bad for once thinking ill of him at those first café encounters. But what was a girl to think when he sent mixed messages?

'I thought I could make it up to you

for running you off the road and Barbara's rudeness the other week.'

His mother should be making apologies herself, Jennifer thought.

'I'm not always the best company. Lots on my mind at the moment, but I'm not making excuses.' It seemed a difficult admission for him.

'Fair enough. Short of selling the cottage to me and making my day, what did you have in mind?'

'Busy this afternoon?'

She paused and held her breath, cautious. 'Actually, I've just finished my shift.'

'So, you're free?' She nodded. 'Since I haven't been back to the area in a while, I thought of taking a spin in the country. I'd enjoy it if you'd care to come along.'

'Would you, now? Interesting.' Naughty of her to stall when he struggled for words. She barely hesitated. What sane woman would? 'I usually don't bother to venture too far on my bike. Too many winding hills and valleys.'

'So, that's a yes?'

'If you promise to watch the speed limit, I might consider it,' she teased.

When he chuckled, she stopped herself from leaping over to give him a hug. 'Absolutely. I'll be an elderly Sunday driver.'

'Nothing more exciting than that?'

'I could ramp it up a notch.'

'Sounds promising.' They were flirting. What a hoot.

'I'll call around to your flat shortly, then?'

Jennifer nodded and glanced down at her work clothes. 'I need to change. Thirty minutes should do it.'

She suddenly felt awkward about being seen with Sam out in front of the café in the street. Danni would tell Olivia. Olivia would tell Sue. This friendship was new and personal and she wanted to keep it private, not have it relayed like a virus on the local grapevine — because she really cared about getting to know this man, although the first time she laid eyes on him she would never have guessed any attraction was possible. It had sure kicked in now. She sighed. Bundilla tongues would wag and gossip flare. Her sensitivity was high and she felt vulnerable.

Then she stopped to think about it more levelly and her mood rose. Good lord, she was going on a date with Sam Keats. Such a small thing, and something to look forward to for a change. A rare treat.

Jennifer cycled furiously home, swiftly changing out of her work clothes, humming with joy. Against her better judgement, she confided in Rachel.

'Sam Keats?' she sneered. 'Bit posh, isn't he?'

Jennifer winced. 'He's a good man.'

'And Boomer isn't?' Rachel retorted.

Jennifer shrugged, deciding to put some tough love into play and tell the truth. 'I'd be aiming higher.'

Rachel snickered. 'New jeans and sweater?' Her critical eye ran over the crisp stone-washed denims and trendy soft black knit.

'You have to wear new clothes for the first time sometime,' she explained. 'It just happens to be today.'

Rachel peered idly down the drive-way. 'Romeo's here. Keen, huh?'

'Oh for heaven's sake, Rachel, give it up.' Jennifer's patience snapped, as she was hurt more than she would ever show by her sister's insults. 'See you later,' she called breezily to her mother, grabbing her bag and heading outside. She would have liked Sam to meet her mother. Rachel was another matter.

Sam was just uncurling his tall frame from his car as she strode to meet him, smiling, her hair down and swinging free, kicked back by the breeze.

'Great timing. I haven't rushed you?'

Jennifer shrugged. 'I can usually be ready to go anywhere in ten minutes.'

'Refreshing.' His absorbing gaze thoroughly checked her over. 'Most women I know feel it's their duty to keep a man waiting.'

He wore the same stylish neat clothes, and his lighter mood encouraged her to relax. When he opened the passenger door, she felt more like a lady than she could remember in a long while. As she slid into her seat and clipped in the seat belt, she watched Sam with pleasure as he strolled around the front of the vehicle to join her. The interior was comfortable and, again, the thought entered her mind that he might have chosen something more luxurious; but from what she knew of him so far, this car accurately reflected him.

It may have been some time since Sam was back in Bundilla, but he certainly remembered his directions, for he confidently took the wheel and headed east from town through the rolling countryside. In spring now, golden drooping racemes of wattle and showers of smaller native thryptomene shrubs were abundant everywhere in the bush to either side, and the eucalyptus forest hugged the verges of the winding road. Where it thinned and cleared, they caught glimpses through dips down to valleys.

After a time, during which their easy silence was unbroken while they both settled into each other's company,

Jennifer said, 'I haven't been out this way in forever. It's so beautiful at this time of year.' She glanced at him. 'I guess you've been at the cottage again today?'

'Mm. But I needed a break. There's a favourite spot I remember up ahead. We'll stop there.'

They pulled up in a roadside viewing area called Ryan's Lookout just below the crest of a hill, with awesome views over a valley, beyond which the terrain flattened out into lush grazing plains. In that far distant scenic pocket, the late afternoon sun slanted its gleaming rays across the tiny patchwork paddocks in varying shades of green.

Jennifer waited, impressed, while this new amiable Sam retrieved a blanket, a bottle of rosé, two wine glasses and a packet of crisps from the boot. They squeezed between the rungs of the wire fence separating the lay-by and a private paddock, and sat down inside on the cool grass, sheltered by the car behind them and lavished with the stunning view.

★ ★ ★

A light breeze swept up from the gully as Sam settled himself on the tartan rug beside his companion. Jennifer Hale was a golden ray of sunshine who had unexpectedly entered his life at the most God-awful moment in time. After he finished clearing the cottage, he hadn't planned on returning to Bundilla. Possibly never again, and definitely not for a long time. Not after the recent bombshell and previous plans he'd already made.

But here was this pure nugget of golden charm and a bucket load of temptation. What the hell was he doing getting interested in a minister's daughter, anyway? He of all people, who in the past had always been attracted by luscious long legs and short skirts rather than the likes of the charming and wispy soul alongside him now? This woman was inexperienced and drew out the need in him for protection, which contradicted her forward and chatty personality. Hardly the shy retiring offspring one might expect from a religious family and upbringing. She had a way about her of forcing you to respond just because she came across as so natural and open with people.

Although she had caught his eye at first sight, he wasn't proud that he hadn't treated Jennifer well in the beginning, so he aimed to make up for it. With his mind more cleared now as he adjusted to the altered circumstances of his life, he felt able to move on.

Sam opened the wine but hesitated before pouring. 'I wasn't sure what your taste might be, or that you even like or drink wine, but this is a late harvest Sauterne. Probably on the sweeter side. I hope you like it.'

Jennifer nodded enthusiastically. 'It sounds lovely.'

Sam was relieved by her warm response because he found he wanted to please this woman — he sought her approval, in a way — and, for some reason, he didn't want to disappoint her as he clearly must have done before.

He poured them each a glass, recapped the bottle and said, 'Dig in,' opening the bag of crisps and offering it to her.

'Wonderfully imaginative of you. My stomach was beginning to complain after a long shift in the café and only a salad for lunch.' She dived a hand into the packet of nibbles.

Before she tasted the wine, she half turned and raised her glass. 'What shall we drink to?'

Good question. What would he like to toast at this point in his life? Right about now, what did he hanker for? 'Contentment,' was the first sentiment that came to mind to help overcome the recent turmoil in his head.

'Deep.' She smiled softly. 'It's not always easily achieved. To contentment then.' She touched his glass with her own and took her first sip. He waited for her reaction.

'Most pleasant,' she decided with an approving nod, then threw his calm by asking, 'Do you mean you *have* contentment, or you're seeking it?'

'The latter,' he admitted.

She was silent for a moment; then, without looking at him, said with soft generosity, 'Then I hope you find it.'

'Thank you. I'm sure it will come. In time.'

'Is that part of the reason why you can't sell the cottage?'

He noticed her use of the word 'can't' as opposed to 'won't'. He knew she was candid, but her comment made him take a mental step back. 'Yeah, I guess so.'

'What are your plans for it then?' she probed further.

The woman sure was frank. After the intrigues of recent weeks, it was a refreshing change. He liked her approach. He respected openness and honesty. It said a lot about a person's character. It took a moment before he could answer. How the hell did he explain? He was just getting used to the new situation himself. He squinted out across the valley.

Sleek black cattle grazed in the nearest grassy paddocks sloping away from them toward a small farm and homestead nestled lower.

'I'd like to hold onto it a while longer, that's all. I'm in no rush to sell,' was the best he could do. To lighten the mood between them that seemed to have turned rather serious, he turned a devilish glance in her direction. 'You're not schmoozing me to get the cottage, are you?' he grinned, grabbing another handful of chips and munching them.

She chuckled. 'No, I do actually like you for yourself. But you do only release tiny teasing bits of information. I suspect there's a lot more to know about Grace, too.'

Sam delayed speaking about her by topping up their wine. Maybe if he forced himself and shared, he would find it easier. 'She lived in Bundilla most of her adult life and I still think of the cottage as her home even though she never owned it. I think that's why I'm actually finding it difficult letting go.'

Jennifer immediately turned those soft blue eyes on him and her voice gentled from teasing to sympathetic. 'Of course you must. Now I feel selfish and pushy for wanting to take advantage of your situation. Your family has strong connections as friends of Grace.'

He nodded. 'She wasn't actually, but from childhood I always called her Auntie,' he reflected. He gained the impression Jennifer knew she was treading on sensitive ground, but she would never guess the reason why. He was still deeply touched by Grace's loss, but her gentle probing was not invasive. For her part, he sensed she needed to know because of her interest in the cottage and, by association, with Grace because she had lived there for so many years.

Sam mentally braced himself for more questions in the course of the conversation. Jennifer had no idea what had just played out in his life with no expectations of him. Her queries came from genuine interest. Maybe it was the reason he felt so comfortable around her and could easily talk.

'Where was Grace from, do you know?' Jennifer asked now.

'A dairy farming family further north on the Murray River.'

'Did she have any siblings?'

'Just the one brother as far as I know. He stayed on the farm.'

Another future quest, to find his uncle William mentioned so liberally in Grace's diaries. On purpose? Had she wanted Sam to know of her brother one day?

'Grace's story is quite touching really, and bound up with Mel and Barbara, but no more so than a lot of relationships during any war when the love of your life is sent away. You hope and pray for their safe return but no one can predict what the future holds. Grace and Barbara were army nurses when the Vietnam War erupted,' he started explaining. 'I always thought it amazing that two such refined ladies should be drawn to such a career.'

Jennifer flashed him a look of surprise, clearly interested in Sam's story and where it was leading, but remained silent.

'After the first Australian troops were sent over, they established a base in Vung Tau, a deep water port in South Vietnam. Ideal for ships to bring in troops. The area had a well-equipped hospital to support the RAAF and other service units, and it was the first port of arrival where supplies and mail came. Because it was already a popular resort before the war, it was used by Australian and American servicemen as a rest area. Also, during their tour it was somewhere to escape on leave and convalesce. They patronised cafés and bars in town. In the tropical heat, of course, the beach was a popular swimming place.'

'Our generation aren't always fully informed about that war. It was our parents' era,' Jennifer said.

'No, and it was a controversial decision that the government of the time made the decision to send troops to support America, who were siding with the South Vietnamese against the communist north. Nui Dat, further up the east coast, became the Australians' task force base because it was in the middle of Viet Cong territory. It became home to thousands of Australian personnel, but mostly they were away on operations patrolling the jungle and camps to drive out the enemy.

'You can imagine,' Sam continued, 'the countryside was heavily vegetated rubber plantations and jungle. And being open fields, the rice paddies were dangerous to cross. Weather must have been a challenge, too. The heat of the dry season or sopping wet in the monsoon.' He paused. 'Enter a young soldier named Peter Charlton, who was with his battalion on its first tour,' Sam ended quietly.

'How long was that?'

'A year.'

'That probably seemed like a long time in a war.'

Sam nodded. 'I'll bet they counted down the days. He was injured and sent out on a medivac helicopter flight to the

RAAF base in Malaysia. If they were assessed as stable enough for the long trip home, they were flown to the Richmond base west of Sydney.'

'Ah.' Jennifer smiled. 'Is that where he met Grace?'

'Yep. By then Barbara had met Mel while he was in Sydney on a business trip. He swept her off her feet. He was older and had worked hard already to establish his building company. Quite the successful man. I gather Barbara came from a family of professionals and her parents disapproved of her choice. Considered him blue collar.'

'Good for her. She followed her heart.'

'So they married and came to live here in Bundilla. From what Mel and Barbara have told me, Peter Charlton was quite a larrikin charmer, completely smitten with young nurse Grace Evans, but his battalion was sent for a second tour of duty so he asked her to write. They started up a correspondence after he was shipped out again. They continued writing to each other for the year he knew he'd be away.'

Sam didn't mention the bundle of letters, preciously saved all these years, that he had recently read with a mixture of fascination and grief.

When he paused in his recounting, Jennifer whispered, 'He was killed, wasn't he?'

Sam nodded.

'Oh how dreadful,' she breathed. 'I couldn't imagine losing the man I loved and being cheated of a lifetime's happiness in such a way.'

'Wars cause so much misery and often serve little justifiable purpose,' he agreed soberly. 'In the case of Vietnam, sadly the communists won. Bitter outcome for everyone involved.'

'You have to wonder what it all achieved.' She sighed and turned to him. 'How do you know all this?'

Sam winced at Jennifer's innocent question. It had been difficult actually untying the string, carefully sliding each of Peter's personal letters to Grace from its envelope and unfolding it to read, feeling as though he was invading her privacy yet needing to know.

'Since I've learned more about him by reading his letters, I've done research on the internet.'

'What happened to him?' Jennifer asked softly.

He took a moment to gather his composure. 'When a soldier was killed, the family had the choice of having him repatriated back here or not. Grace wasn't listed as his next of kin so she had no say. Peter's family opted for a burial in a military cemetery in Malaysia.' He paused. 'I found an engagement ring among Grace's possessions.'

Jennifer gasped. 'No way! Peter was her fiancé?' When Sam nodded, she continued in a rush, 'Oh that's wonderful, and yet it's worse.'

Sam wasn't ready to reveal everything. The information was still too raw.

'Grace and Peter were unlucky in love,' Jennifer said quietly with compassion.

Sam let out a deep slow sigh. 'So,

Grace lost the man she loved, and I gather Barbara and Mel decided to help her. He had already begun investing in property, which included this cottage, so he generously let her come and stay. I gather it was only meant to be temporary, but it ended up becoming permanent.'

Sam knew so much more remained unsaid, and while he felt it easy to open his heart to this sparkling genuine woman and confide in her, he was still travelling the journey of early discovery himself and needed more time.

Beside him, Jennifer shivered in the rising breeze and hugged her knees, their wine glasses empty now, crisps eaten.

'I can't deny I'm not disappointed about the cottage,' she admitted. 'But after hearing Grace's story today, I fully appreciate your connection to it now.' She turned to him. 'Thank you for sharing.'

He managed a grin to help cover his conflict inside. 'You're an understanding listener.' He had divulged way more than he intended, but Jennifer was a willing ear and, somehow, just sitting out here away from the memories had helped clear his mind.

'Bundilla's a small town with a reasonably settled population,' Jennifer said, 'so it's not overloaded with houses coming onto the market — which John Parker verified, so I'm not exactly filled with hope or cheer that a similar property will appear any time soon.' She frowned and spoke, as if to herself. 'I suppose I could consider buying elsewhere.'

The possibility surprised him. 'Not stay in Bundilla? Since you want to buy the cottage so desperately I assumed — '

'You're right. I'm teasing,' she chuckled. 'Five years ago when we moved here, we had no idea how Bundilla would grow so deeply in all of us. It's so warm and welcoming, such a caring community. And when Dad became ill, the thoughtfulness and concern and medical support was wonderfully reassuring and support-ive. Dad, of course, had such a strong faith, utterly accepting of his fate and unafraid to die. An inspiration.'

'So you stayed on?'

She nodded and huddled further into herself against the freshening wind drifting up the hillside. 'At secondary school in my teens I hated leaving friends every few years when Dad was offered another ministry. He'd consult with us all and pray about his decision, but usually we ended up leaving and heading for a new town. I know it was his life's work, but we'd have to make new friends all over again. As much as we all promised each other to stay in touch, inevitably I lost contact with all my former girlfriends. Each time, I grew more frustrated. I mean, I make friends easily enough and we learnt to adapt over the years, but it was still a huge wrench.'

Jennifer paused for a moment, reflective. 'So when Bundilla opened up its arms to us as a family and fully embraced us, I decided then and there to stay. I dug my toes in. I didn't even contemplate university because, honestly,' she glanced across at him a touch self consciously, 'I had no idea what I really wanted to do. I loved organising and I'd helped Dad with parish work so it seemed logical to look into a clerical career. Stewart Dalton had retired but after his wife died, he returned to legal practice. I came along just at the right time. He advertised for a legal secretary and I got the job. He works an easy week.' She grinned. 'As you saw in his office, there's just Stewart; our receptionist junior, Natalie Gardner; and myself. He's tried to find another lawyer to buy the practice, but no luck so far. It's always difficult attracting people away from the cities, where they have everything, compared to the simpler life and isolation of smaller country towns.

'David Ormond came as Vicar into the manse to take over the parish, and Sue Parker, bless her, took over the café. It expanded and she needed more staff so I applied for weekend shifts.'

'What other family do you have besides Rachel? You mentioned brothers.'

'Three.' She held up the same number of fingers. 'I'm the oldest, Rachel is the youngest, and the boys are all in between. Adam is a Flying Doctor pilot in outback Queensland mostly. It's all he ever wanted to do. Joshua is the middle one. He's a mechanic in Castlemaine and every spare moment he's restoring an old vintage Studebaker. He rents a house with mates. And then there's Luke. He took after our father and is studying for the ministry in Adelaide. He's the quiet one but he has a whacky sense of humour.'

They sat in silence for a while, the day still lovely but chilling off toward evening. The peaceful countryside wrapped its silence about them.

'It's not like this in the city,' Sam said eventually. 'There's always traffic and noise and movement.'

'Well, hard to escape it in Melbourne. Do you look forward to weekends?'

'At the moment, yes. But Bundilla's been a double-edged escape really.

137

Great to get back here again but poignant too for many reasons.'

'I imagine.'

'So what's it's like being a minister's daughter?'

'Not you, too,' she chided in her deep, soft voice that acquired an edge of playful exasperation. 'Everyone expects you to be a saint but I'll let you in on a secret.' She lowered her voice and leaned closer. 'I don't plan on becoming a nun.'

'Praise the Lord.'

They both burst out laughing.

'What about you?' she asked while her clear blue eyes still sparkled. 'No brothers or sisters?'

He shook his head. 'Only child.'

Jennifer looked at him with compassion. 'Poor Sam,' she murmured.

He shrugged off her sentiment, not seeking self-pity. 'Mel and Barbara wanted me to have a private education so I was sent off to boarding school in Melbourne when I was ten, but I had plenty of mates. Then I transitioned straight into university. So, as far as I'm concerned,

138

the city's been my home most of my life.'

The sun finally lost its battle and slid below the top of the surrounding hills, casting them into shadow and stealing any shreds of remaining warmth. Reluctantly, Sam decided it was time to make a move and head back to town. He stood up and extended a hand, offering to help Jennifer rise.

'Your hands are freezing,' he said as he gripped them and pulled her up. He kept hold of them and gently rubbed them between his own. 'Thanks for understanding about my not selling the cottage.'

'Just remember, if you ever put it on the market, you sell to me, okay?' she cautioned lightly.

The sight of her large blue eyes glittering at him in her creamy wholesome face almost took his breath away, and he wondered how such a fragile little thing, so unlike any other woman he had ever been drawn to, could so completely capture his full attention.

'I believe I might.' He hesitated. 'I've enjoyed today.'

'Me, too.'

Still holding her hands, he gently tugged her closer. 'We should do it again,' he suggested.

'If you want.'

'I want,' he murmured, then gave up resisting her expectant upturned face and tasted the rosy lips just below his, begging to be kissed.

One wasn't enough, of course, so he returned for seconds, releasing their handhold and sliding his arms around her waist, drawing her warm and tight against him. They explored each other and deepened the kiss while he thrilled to her full response. This woman sure was no saint. She gave her emotions full rein, completely and honestly. He nurtured their embrace and first exploration of each other but after the initial rush subsided, he eased back and they drew apart.

Their mutual attraction spoke volumes, so there was no need for words.

In silence, he gathered up their picnic and they scrambled back through the fence to the car. On the winding drive from the hills and down into Bundilla again to Jennifer's flat, neither of them spoke. The undercurrent between them had simmered since they met but fizzed into life today like someone striking a match.

'Back to civilisation,' Sam said as he drew up outside Jennifer's flat. 'Thanks for a great afternoon.'

'You're welcome.'

'See you next weekend?'

'Might not be free much.' She wrinkled her nose. 'With the weather warming up, tourists are increasing. Café's getting busier, which means longer working hours. Sue likes to keep it open as long as there are customers.'

'Fair enough.' He shrugged. 'Play it by ear, then?'

He thought she might back off for all the same reasons that bothered him, so he was relieved to hear they might get the chance to connect again. He had to leave early tomorrow and there was little chance he could see her again before her shift ended. He would miss her company. Besides, between Grace's letter from Peter and other revelations, he needed some space.

Although it would not nearly suffice enough to last him the whole week, he leaned across to Jennifer. His intentions were clear. Her eyes softened and she met him halfway, their kiss a lingering union of two willing souls.

As he drove away, Sam knew they had started something that seemed destined to be fraught with difficulty. He lived in Melbourne. Jennifer was entrenched in Bundilla. For the moment, with freeways and modern cars, distance could be overcome — but as to the future? She was a decent, passionate woman who drew him like a magnet. He'd need to be careful with his heart. It was all becoming a bit interesting and tricky.

★ ★ ★

The next day, to Jennifer's disappointment, she didn't hear from Sam at all. After their wonderful few hours together yesterday afternoon and that wow of a goodbye before they parted, she thought he might at least have phoned or tried to make contact of some kind before he left. His car was at the cottage, of course, as she expected when she pedalled past on her way to the café, and she eyed it longingly with a dull ache. A whole week without him. Cruel. She pulled her hopes back into place. He was a city bloke and she was established here.

The week dragged without Sam and she had another argument with Rachel, who still had no job.

'I need your contribution, Rachel,' Jennifer pleaded. 'I need your money now.'

'I don't have any. I spent it.'

'Your job-seeking allowance? All of it?'

She was willing to bet Rachel was not seriously looking for work at all. The girl was so troubled, Jennifer felt baffled as to how she would help guide her back on track.

Rachel dug in her jeans pocket and drew out a crumpled ten-dollar note. She tossed it at her sister, but because Jennifer wasn't expecting it, the money floated to the floor.

Jennifer bent to pick it up and said quietly, 'Your share is way more than that, Rachel, and you know it. I contribute half and you and mum share the other half from your welfare.' Knowing matters in the household were coming to a crunch, she laid down an ultimatum to her sister. 'Pay your share regularly on pay day and on time from now on, or you're out.'

Jennifer grew sick in the stomach at having uttered such words and sounded so heartless, even if she hadn't meant them, but Rachel had to learn. Their situation couldn't continue. Her sister had grown disrespectful and out of control. Headstrong, she listened to no one.

So by the following weekend Jennifer was desperate to catch up with David for another counselling session. They kept it casual, often over a meal. During what her sore feet told her had been a frantic day in the café the following Saturday, Jennifer left work later than usual and went straight around to David, cycling by the flat first and checking their phone for any messages.

Rose gave her a teasing smile. 'Nothing from Sam, dear.'

Jennifer felt herself blush to think she had been so transparent and moved the conversation forward. 'Rachel home?'

Her mother's look of despair supplied the answer. 'I feel I should be doing more to help.' She frowned in distress.

'Well, Sue has suggested tough love. I'll see what David recommends tonight. I'm lost, too, Mum,' she admitted, on the verge of tears. 'You can't force an adult to do something against their will even when you know it's for their own benefit.'

'I'll keep praying, but maybe our Rachel will only learn by making mistakes.'

'Life can be a hard teacher,' Jennifer agreed.

Still troubled over her sister, thoughts of Sam in the back of her mind and not having heard from him, she took comfort in knowing she could offload to David, and quickly changed into casual clothes.

'Not sure how long I'll be.' She kissed her mother fondly and left for the manse.

The large white timber house with verandas all around and latticework trim had been the lovely big family home where she had lived with her father until his death last year when David took over as vicar and moved in. As she wheeled her bike up the driveway and leant it against a veranda post, she inhaled drifts of perfume from the row of lavender all along the fence, feeling a tug of nostalgia, but no resentment that she and Rachel had been left homeless. The manse belonged to the church, so her parents had never owned their own home: the very reason she sought the security of one for herself, regardless of the fact that she was single, unattached and not planning to marry any time soon. The dream of home ownership was solely for her mother.

She took the familiar steps up to the front door, loudly wielding the brass knocker. When David didn't immediately respond, she rapped again, longer and harder. It took a few minutes but he eventually appeared in jeans and a sweater, looking vague.

'Jennifer.' They embraced warmly. 'Apologies for not answering sooner. Working on my sermon.'

'Sorry to interrupt.'

'No, no,' he said generously. 'I was expecting you.'

'Thanks for seeing me again.'

'I know you're worried about Rachel. Rose okay?'

Jennifer nodded. 'She's heating up a frozen meal. I hinted I might be a while.'

'Mrs. Daley gave me a lamb roast that I don't know what to do with,' he hinted as she followed him down the broad hallway.

Jennifer caught David's helpless grin flung casually with a brief backward glance over his shoulder.

'Fake,' she chuckled. 'You know your way around a kitchen.' She shook her head and conceded. 'Sure. Be nice cooking in a decent big kitchen again.' She sighed, appreciating the gorgeous vicar with his cheeky grin and sense of humour. They had clicked from day one. As mates. 'What you need is a good woman. You're too independent.'

'She'll happen along.'

David swept an arm about in a flourish. 'Listen, this has worked out well. I could use a break from being stuck in the study all afternoon. How about a spin on the bike? A bit of unwinding before we talk?'

Jennifer's mood lifted. A run on the road on his motorcycle? She was there. 'Love to. Can I just check your refrigerator first, though, in case we need to pick up anything while we're out? Unless you're all sorted on the food front,' she teased.

He often dined on the hospitality of his parishioners and coped in the kitchen, but shopping was not a strong point.

David's handsome face eased into a smile and revealed his engaging dimple. 'You know me too well. Go check while I get the gear.'

As he headed in another direction toward the back porch where he kept his kit, Jennifer glanced around the familiar huge country kitchen, eaten up with envy: miles of counter-top, an island bench, and the butler's sink beneath the window with its awesome view out over the back garden. The old stuffed sofa still sat at the far end of the room. She chose to forget how many unhappy dinners their family had shared in tense silence sitting around the big table.

Laying her poor memories aside, Jennifer poked her head into fridge and freezer, opened the crisper and sighed with relief. Enough vegetables to go with the meat, which she quickly transferred into a covered baking dish to start cooking while they were out on their ride.

When David reappeared from the porch at the other end of the kitchen, laden with helmets and protective leathers and seeing Jennifer bustling about his kitchen, he grinned. 'I've been invited out a lot the last few days.' He shrugged. 'Haven't had a chance to get to it.'

'Fibber,' she teased. 'You were waiting for me to come around and cook it, weren't you?'

He rearranged the gear more comfortably in his arms. 'You don't have other plans for tonight, do you?'

'No, of course not.' It hurt Jennifer to admit it and working seven days a week, people had grown to expect that she had little time or interest in a social life. 'No hot date,' she joked to cover her disappointment thinking of Sam, and plastered a false smile across her face for David's benefit. 'Except with you. Honestly David, if you weren't destined to move parishes every few years, I'd marry you and jump your bones.'

He threw back his head and laughed. 'I accept that as a huge compliment.'

'Thank goodness I'm done with constantly moving. I just want to stay put.'

David set down his spare helmet and a thickly padded black parka. 'Put these on and I'll fire up the bike and bring it around to the front.'

Jennifer tried to stay cheerful as she walked back down the hallway with the helmet under her arm to wait for David. She couldn't help wondering why Sam hadn't made contact. Was he beavering away, engrossed in the cottage, or was her interpretation of the heat between them last Sunday only in her own hopeful imagination?

As she leaned on the white picket fence, she heard the deep throbbing motor of David's Honda kick into life. She clipped on her helmet as it rumbled down the driveway at the side of the house, David looking cool in his usual black leather battle jacket and helmet, too. He had almost convinced her to invest in a small motor scooter to replace her bicycle. Faster and more comfortable, inexpensive to buy and run, he had argued — the reason he had bought a motor bike for a few years while saving for a small car on his modest salary.

Jennifer knew the handsome and unattached new vicar was great husband potential. But there was no chemistry or spark. They often joked about it. They had become close mates, but Jennifer only saw David as her vicar and a valued friend, an all-round fun bloke who loved his calling and breathed joy into everyone he met . . . unlike her father, ranting and inflexible, repressing his family; then sitting across the desk in his parish office from naïve parishioners, dishing out righteous plaudits for them to live by, when his own family life was a sham.

When David stopped the bike beside her, she swung her leg over behind him and wrapped her arms around him tight. It was not the first time he had treated her to the exhilaration of the open road.

'Ready?' David half turned to yell at her over the engine.

'Yep.'

He gunned the accelerator on the handlebar, wove along the two streets until they met the southern highway out of town, and powered up to speed. It had been a while since she'd ridden with David and she'd almost forgotten the elation and release of feeling the breeze whipping by, the glorious freedom of the open road. More than breezy enough to blow away any cobwebs of doubt in her mind over Sam and learn to take each day as it came.

They just rode. The bottom ends of her long hair flipped back in the wind. The bike hummed beneath them with its sexy power. David was probably mulling over the details of tomorrow morning's sermon. As the early evening shadows lengthened, he raised an arm and twirled his hand to let her know they were slowing to turn around and head back to town.

The quiet streets of Bundilla opened up before them until David indicated, and they pulled to a stop in front of the manse. Jennifer hopped off, unstrapped her helmet and shook her long hair free. 'Thanks for the ride. It's as good as a dose of medicine, isn't it?' She gave David a quick hug of appreciation. As she did so, she glimpsed a familiar silver vehicle cruise along the street. Sam! Jennifer's face spread into a wide smile of pleasure and she instinctively waved to him. He returned the gesture but drove on. Jennifer's heart dropped with rejection. Maybe he was on his way to somewhere else. Suddenly, she felt powerless. And she wouldn't be at the flat if he phoned — at least, not until later tonight. She was committed to an evening with David. She couldn't just eat and run. She heaved an anxious sigh of resignation and marched indoors to check the roast.

Jennifer barely focused on David's easy conversation as she set the table and added vegetables to the pan, because she was so preoccupied with thinking of Sam. Would he be at the cottage alone, thinking she was fickle with her affections? Did he not know her well enough yet to believe she didn't care? He wouldn't know that David wasn't her boyfriend. She could imagine what it must have looked like: returning his kiss one weekend and flirting with someone else the next.

Guilt gnawed away at her inner peace all evening that Sam might misjudge her until she explained — hopefully before he returned to Melbourne, otherwise he would feel deceived.

'This house always feels so much like a family home,' Jennifer admitted later when she pushed her regrets aside.

'Some houses have that feel about them,' David agreed.

'Yes, they do, don't they?' She smiled across at him, immediately thinking of Grace's cottage.

'Generous of you to say so when I know the manse doesn't have the best memories for you.'

He reached over and squeezed her hand as they sat drinking huge mugs of hot tea after dinner, eating chocolate fudge biscuits one of his church ladies had baked. Comfort food. David's touch was only a gentle token of kindness, but it was almost her undoing in the light of her joint emotional distraction this evening: worry for Rachel's future, and anxiety over the standing of her serious attraction to Sam Keats.

David eased the conversation around to Rachel. 'What's going on in her mind right now isn't necessarily something she can share.'

'But is it okay for adults to rebel like that when life isn't working?'

David shrugged. 'She needs to get her confusion out of her system. Head off on a path of her own to find that whole other person she'll eventually be.'

'She's not making any effort in any direction at the moment,' Jennifer complained.

'Maybe she just hasn't found the right solution yet. She'll be testing everything; traditions as she's known them. Clearly small town life isn't working for her, so don't be surprised if an opportunity arises and she takes it.'

'Leaves Bundilla, you mean?'

'Possibly. Don't be shocked if it happens.'

'Personally I can't see it. She has no goals whatsoever and expects others to take all the responsibility.'

David shrugged. 'She might fail, even admit she was wrong, but experience is a valuable re-creation tool.' He assessed her closely for a moment.

Jennifer moved uncomfortably. 'Whatever you have to say I can take it,' she muttered, grinning.

He waited a moment before he began. 'Are you sure your expectations of Rachel at the moment aren't too rigid? To her, you might be sounding like your father.'

Jennifer gasped. 'Heaven forbid.'

'I know you feel fully responsible for her while your mother's still unwell, but do you really need to control her so tightly? Maybe just support her more as she's going through this phase.'

'A phase, you think?' Jennifer felt hopeful that this horrid time in her sister's life might not last.

'More than likely. Even in my short time in the ministry I've seen many lost souls stray but find their way back.'

'She seems to be so unhappy with everything right now.'

'And she's taking it out on those closest around her, right?'

Jennifer nodded.

'My suggestion? Back off. Let her go. That's the hardest part.'

'How can I do that? She'll think I don't care.'

'She knows. Just watch out for her from a distance. You just might have to accept that Rachel's life and path may be different than your own or what you want for her.'

A comfortable silence settled between them for a while as Jennifer considered David's advice. 'Rachel took the brunt of father's discipline because she was the most defiant.'

'Disapproval breeds rebellion,' David said.

'We had plenty of that from our father,' Jennifer muttered.

'I can understand Rachel wanting to stand up for herself since his death. She has no limits, no barriers, no hard discipline. Seems to me like she's breaking out. Pushing boundaries and finding her way.'

'Well she better find it soon because she has little or no money, stays at home and resists every suggestions at every turn. Do you think it's insecurity and she doesn't have the courage to move on?'

'Or know how,' David suggested.

Yawning and weary from the strain of talking, Jennifer stretched in the cosiness and warmth of the heated room. She checked the time. 'That late already? I should go.'

'Thanks for dinner, Jen. You're a great cook.' David rose and gave her a reassuring hug.

'You're welcome. And thank you for

the advice. Wise words as always. Your perspective is impartial and unclouded. You've helped. I appreciate it.'

'I can walk back to the flat with you,' he suggested.

She shook her head. 'I'll be fine. Night.'

He waved in response, standing in the open front doorway, backlit by the indoor lights. She hopped on her bike and cycled, with a new healing resolution and sense of purpose, back to the flat. It was in darkness, Rose obviously in bed. Her hopeful glance toward the telephone revealed no flashing messages on the answering machine. Not from Sam and certainly not from Rachel, both clearly occupied elsewhere tonight. Jennifer wasn't sure which one hurt her the most.

5

To Sam's great annoyance, he had only been informed late last night of an urgent and important meeting in his city architectural office hastily scheduled for this morning, so his return to Bundilla was delayed. He'd barely concentrated throughout as he and his fellow partners worked through their agenda, impatient to be on the highway and heading inland. So instead of arriving Friday night as usual, he had not driven into town until early this afternoon. He had sat in the car and immediately phoned Jennifer's number at the flat from his mobile in the hope she might be home, but there was no answer. So he had driven around to Sue's café, trusting he would find her still at work, only to discover that the owner was closing up and the subject of his pursuit had already left.

The café owner had eyed him with interest and when he asked after Jennifer, her eyes sparkled and she was most obliging.

'I think she was heading for the manse next door to the little bluestone church. Big white house in Duncan Street.'

He smiled his thanks and sped off in the appropriate direction. He had spied Jennifer and the young vicar together. Easing herself lithely off the back of a gleaming black motor bike, she had looked lithe and wild, especially when she shook out her hair and combed her fingers through it after lifting off the helmet. Quite a coup. A vicar with a chick magnet. Who knew? Then she had smiled at the man and they had hugged. He wished he'd taken his time. That way he would have missed them.

In that moment, Sam knew he was jealous. Since coming to Bundilla for weekends, he had actually stopped long enough in his frantic city life to find time to slow down, in the process finding and socialising with a decent female who wasn't high maintenance for a change. Just a natural energetic woman who turned his head for a second glance right from that first sight of her in the café when she had taken his order and walked away, taking that neat backside and long legs with her. His heart rolled over by a chance meeting with a striking personality he would never have met if not for being compelled to return to town.

Glowering through the tinted windows of his car, his body twisted with resentment to see Jennifer with the vicar. They looked pretty darn cosy with each other. After a couple of meetings and one outing that might remotely be considered a date, he had no reason to be so protective. Then he saw the sense. Minister's daughter. Handsome young vicar. Logical. An ideal match. Except the kisses he had shared with her so far had been far from pure. In fact they had burst with an unexpected passion, heathen and exciting, especially coming from such an innocent trusting creature.

In their few encounters so far he'd grown to actually look forward to coming back to Bundilla each weekend because Jennifer Hale was here. She listened, was uncomplicated company, gorgeous, and always had a happy outlook. Her sunny nature was rubbing off on him. How could he not be affected by such an effervescent personality with such an enthusiasm for life?

She was tall and lithe, athletic, with an appealing nature that equalled her physical grace. She wasn't just attractive, she was utterly beautiful both in looks and character, with an understated sensuality she didn't know she possessed. Her warmth and passion were effortlessly conveyed to everyone around her.

Sam's radar had locked onto hers the first time he'd seen her gliding smoothly between tables in the café. She had swung those slim hips encased in fitted slacks as she breezed about the warm room buzzing with conversation, smiling as she served customers, stopping here and there to chat. It seemed she knew most people but if she worked seven days, she couldn't have much time for a social life. He couldn't criticise. He wasn't much better.

Seeing her with the vicar had given him a jolt of reality. He remembered her warm body and deep kiss from last weekend. Jennifer Hale had crept into his mind and his senses so that he was thinking of taking her into his confidence about Grace because she seemed genuinely interested in learning more about her and the cottage. And he'd reached a place in his mind where he was ready to confide.

Now with the vicar on the scene and doubts rising, he needed to rethink: not only another man on the horizon, but their different lives as well. Simple truth was, small towns made him claustrophobic.

With a sigh of resignation, Sam pushed the natural untamed waves out of his face and heaved yet another cardboard box of memorabilia and keep-sakes out to the car. That was another problem he tussled with at the moment. All this stuff and what it meant.

* * *

In her flat, Jennifer turned on the heater, grabbed the cordless phone and settled into the sofa. She had absolutely nothing to lose by making a few calls. She knew Sam had seen her out in front of the manse dismounting from David's motorbike, but he had taken off and it had bothered her all night. She was deeply disappointed he hadn't stopped, expecting him to at least open one of those mysterious tinted windows in his car and say hello. Better yet, actually get out and come over to chat. She would have loved to introduce him to David.

There was absolutely nothing to be done now if he had left because he mistook her visit with the vicar, but she could try to set the record straight.

She didn't flatter herself that Sam cared enough to be envious of seeing her with another man, but you didn't pash a woman the way they had last weekend and feel something fabulous leap into life with that other person if you felt nothing. Sam didn't come across as the type of man who would use you and dump you. He was too polite for that, and it showed in every single gesture when he treated her like a lady. He was a solid character. All she knew was that Sam was back in town somewhere and they were apart.

So, what to do? She could sit back sedately like an old-fashioned girl and wait until he got in touch, or she could be proactive and phone him first. Not having his mobile number, she decided to phone the Keats residence. It was a long shot ripe for trouble but she lived in hope.

'Hi Barbara, it's Jennifer Hale,' she announced warmly, inhaling a steadying breath. 'I know it's late but I wondered if Sam might be with you?'

If and when he came on the line, she had no idea what she would say, but she just needed to hear his voice again. Foolish for many reasons, but she was beginning to care big time for Sam Keats.

'Sam's not here,' Barbara said crisply, offering no further explanation.

'Do you know where he might be?'

'At the cottage.' Equally blunt.

'Would he be seeing you while he's in town?'

The line fell silent and Jennifer puzzled over her hesitation.

'I doubt it. Sam's very busy at the moment. His time in town at the week-ends is limited.'

'Oh.' He came all the way from the city and didn't visit his parents? 'Would you have his mobile number?'

'No I don't.'

Jennifer panicked for a moment, afraid she might miss him tomorrow before she had a chance to explain. Not to mention feeling stung by Barbara's hostility. The image of a mattress on one of the bedroom floors in the cottage flashed into Jennifer's mind. Sam had admitted he wasn't close to his parents. So sad to think they were estranged or that he wasn't welcome in the family home. He ate in the café sometimes and always alone. A sense of concern welled up inside her for him. Something wasn't right.

'Thank you anyway, Barbara.' Trying to smooth the troubled waters between them, Jennifer added quickly, 'The annual hospital fête was another huge success last week.'

Her tone immediately softened. 'Yes, we raised a record amount this year,' she boasted.

'Largely due to your leadership as chairwoman of the fund raising committee, I'm sure.'

'I enjoy the work and the challenge. It's a worthy cause and someone has to take the lead.'

'Yes. The hospital staff appreciate the extra funding towards equipment. Well,

I must go and see if I can find your son.'

As she hung up, Jennifer wondered if she imagined the gasp on the other end of the phone. She winced. Any parent would be hurt or upset if alienated from their children, and she cursed herself for being so insensitive. Jennifer wondered what had gone wrong in the Keats family.

After her call to Barbara Keats, Jennifer grew desperate. She didn't have Sam's mobile and she wasn't cycling around to the cottage at this hour of the night. Somehow she must find the courage to stop by tomorrow. Unless he contacted her beforehand. She could only hope.

* * *

Jennifer attended the early service in the tiny bluestone church of St. Luke's the following morning before she started work in the café for Sunday brunches. Unlike yesterday, patronage

170

eased off in the afternoon with the arrival of frisky winds and spring showers. The weather pattern of recent warm and sunny days enticing people outdoors, followed by a cool change, would continue throughout spring until the more intense heat of early summer kicked into play.

Having forgotten her showerproof coat this morning with no sign of rain, Jennifer was caught out when she left the café and cycled toward Grace's cottage, fighting a strong breeze and the first drops of rain. She pedalled faster but was still soggy when she jumped off her bike, hastily propping it against the front picket fence and racing for the shelter of the front porch.

She worried for a moment that Sam had already returned to Melbourne or wasn't around, because his car wasn't parked out front as usual — until she glimpsed it beneath blossom trees in what looked like a small orchard behind the house. The property must have rear access. Some of the laneways from the early days of the town still survived.

Jennifer shook off the worst of the drops and raked fingers through her damp tangled hair. It would be dark soon. The light was already fading with heavy rain clouds. She had a light on her bike and wanted to get home to dry off, but she needed to satisfy her compulsion to see Sam and explain. She might make a fool of herself but she rapped on the knocker beside the closed front door anyway. This conversation was either going to be very long or very short. Shivering, she waited and rapped again. She was about to try a third time when she heard footsteps, and the door opened before her raised arm.

'Hi.' She beamed with pleasure at the sight of him. She would not be intimidated by that narrowed gaze. She had come on a mission. To right a misunderstanding.

'I'm surprised to see you,' he grunted.

Sam Keats was adorable when he was unsure. Well, he was pretty much cute most of the time, but especially at the moment. Her heart leapt because she could tell by the tension that seeped out of him that he was jealous, and you were only jealous if you had feelings for someone. The kiss had meant something after all.

Charged with optimism, she asked, 'Why?'

'Thought you were with the vicar.'

He was fishing! She wanted to fling her arms around him and plant a luscious kiss on his mouth. Keep it casual, Jennifer thought. Pretend nothing is wrong.

'Oh, he offered to take me for a ride in payment for cooking dinner. I waved to you. Didn't you see me?' He nodded. 'You should have come over and I would have introduced you.'

'I didn't want to interrupt.'

'David and I?'

She was about to laugh but stopped her reaction at a grin. The scowl on Sam's face was genuine and appealing. He really was offended because he had seen her give David that thank-you hug. She mentally rubbed her hands together. This could go further so she swiftly reassured him.

'I've known him for over a year since he took over Father's parish. We're really good friends and he's been advising me with Rachel. I think of him as a brother,' she hinted softly. When she realised Sam had no idea what she was talking about, Jennifer explained, 'My sister is having a difficult time at the moment.'

Her heart thrilled to see relief cross Sam's shadowed face, and his whole manner changed. His big shoulders relaxed beneath a charcoal thick-knit jumper and he thrust his hands deep into the pockets of his black jeans.

Then concern clouded his expression and he frowned again but for a different reason. 'You're shivering.'

'Yes, it's freezing out now so I won't hold you up. I'm sure you have lots to do. Knowing you were back in town, I just wanted to say hello.' What else could she say, short of inviting herself in? She had already dispelled any confusion.

'That all?' His voice went all soft and husky.

She hesitated but only for the slightest moment before leaning toward him and suggesting, 'Unless you're offering more . . . hospitality.'

He chuckled — a deep sexy rumble in his throat, accompanied by a devastating grin that edged up those lovely lips she had kissed last weekend.

'I have a fire going inside. Let's get you dry.' He gestured behind him and stepped aside, then closed the door behind them, and she gratefully followed him down the hall for a chance to dry out and warm up before she rode home.

'I didn't have your number so I phoned your mother . . . '

He startled her when he whirled around suddenly and stopped. Jennifer was only aware that his unexpected movement brought them so close she could see the light flecks of gold in his dark brown eyes and feel his warm breath flush her face.

'What for?'

'To find out where on earth you were, silly,' she teased. 'Unless you don't want to be found.'

'Only by you,' he whispered, sliding a supportive and comforting arm about her waist and drawing her close against him.

When he kissed her long and tenderly, she didn't want it to end. Her damp clothes clung to his muscled warmth then her arms slid up around his neck.

'That's a relief,' she breathed with heady delight when they both reluctantly parted.

This man was rapidly seeping into her soul, but there were all kinds of pitfalls and complications looming to heartache. But you couldn't ignore feelings this strong. She planned to at least see where they led. She pushed out a long gentle sigh of frustration. Plot and plan had always been her motto, but that proved useless when fate had other ideas.

'Come on.' He sought her hand and

drew her further on. 'It's warmer down the back.'

'Typical spring day. Started out fine then turned miserable.' Jennifer covered her uncertainty with forced brightness, feeling a deeper connection flowing through her than their linked hands.

'Oh, I'd say it's turned out exactly the way I like.' He flashed her a devilish grin.

Wow, he really was pulling out all the stops. 'Pleased to hear I'm not intruding. I don't usually gatecrash.'

'Liar,' he said softly. 'You said that last time.' He grew serious and leant down to steal another tender kiss that buckled her knees, so she clung to him and made it last. 'Maybe we can get to know each other better.'

'I think we're already on the way, don't you?' she murmured.

He grinned and tugged her through the door into what, on her previous visit, had been a lovely sunny room. This evening, with descending darkness and scudding clouds bringing broken drifts of soaking rain outside, the kitchen and living area was a cosy cocoon of warmth from a single lamp and flickering flames from the open fire at the far end.

Even more furniture was missing since last weekend except for a comfy sofa, recliner chair and television, plus a small side table piled with books. The room was welcoming and snug in the fire's dancing glow.

Drawn toward the flames, Jennifer moved to the hearth, held out her cold hands and said, 'Something smells wonderful.'

'Just vegetable soup. Let's get you dry first, then eat.'

'Oh, I didn't plan to — '

'No arguments. You're staying for dinner.'

Jennifer's mind raced. No way would she refuse such a tempting invitation, but she must contact her mother so she didn't worry. 'Do you mind if I make a call first?' She looked around for the phone and spied it on the wall.

Sam shook his head. 'Go ahead. I'll fetch a towel for your hair.'

He discreetly left while Jennifer awkwardly explained that she was waiting out the rain and might not be home for a while.

'Thank you for letting me know, dear,' Rose said. 'Take care.' An amused warmth of intuition entered her voice. Cheered and relieved by her unspoken understanding and perception, Jennifer made a note to give her mother a hug later.

When Sam returned, she knelt on the rug, did as she was told, and lapped up the indulgence of being spoiled. It had been such a long time since anyone had fussed over her like this. With her head bent toward the drying flames, Jennifer couldn't see what Sam was doing as she towelled her damp hair but heard him cross to the kitchen. Sounded like he was unscrewing a bottle top.

'Do you drink brandy?'

She managed a side glance over her shoulder. 'Absolutely.' She helped him over the awkward moment. 'I haven't only drunk altar wine at communion, you know. We shared a whole bottle of lovely wine last weekend, remember?' she said dryly, amused by this confident man's discretion.

He handed her a small brandy balloon and they clinked glasses.

'I thought a snifter of spirits might help warm you up quicker.'

The fiery sip of auburn liquid creamed its way down her throat. 'To a cosy night in.' Jennifer groaned. 'I hope the weather eases up a bit or I'll get drenched riding home.'

'You can stay the night.'

When her gaze widened and her lips rounded in surprise, he held up a hand and grinned.

'No strings,' he clarified. 'There are plenty of bedrooms. I've never jumped a woman I've just met.'

As long as you do at some stage, that would be wonderful, Jennifer thought, scandalised as her mind leapt ahead to some possible time in the future. It was impossible not to consider Sam Keats in an entirely new light now. Handsome. Gorgeous smile. And, she suspected, lonely. Which only brought out her feminine instinct to nurture.

'Most gentlemanly of you.' She set her glass on the hearth and continued towelling her hair. 'I know I'm probably prying but I'll ask anyway,' she said gently. 'Is the situation with your parents so bad you must stay here in the cottage?' She cringed as the words left her mouth and glanced across at him for his reaction.

He heaved a deep sigh, sprawled on the rug beside her, leaning back on one arm and unhurriedly swirling his amber drink before taking a long sip.

'It's a long story,' he said eventually after staring into the flames. 'Which I shall tell you after dinner if you'd care to listen.'

'Only if you're comfortable,' she explained.

'I appreciate your concern. I don't know many people in town these days enough to stop and have a chat. I've been away far longer than I've ever lived here. Although one or two of my primary school peers still around are starting to remember me since I've been returning the past few weekends and actually recognise me enough to greet me on the street.'

'In a small place like Bundilla, the locals all know a stranger or new face in town.'

'And word spreads.'

She nodded and they shared a smile.

Sam had been right. The brandy was blissfully warming and her hair quickly dried. By the time it was dark, he was spooning soup into deep bowls and placed triangles of buttered Vegemite toast on a plate which he set between them in front of the fire on the floor.

They sat cross-legged and started their soup.

'Very tasty,' Jennifer commended.

'I've had years of bachelor practice.'

'What else do you like to cook?'

'Not much,' he admitted sheepishly.

'Whatever's on the menu in a restaurant or looks enticing among all those fake cardboard box cover photographs on frozen meals.'

Jennifer's heart went out to him again, but her reasoning was edged with caution. No man with Sam's good looks and latent appeal would be eating alone too often. All the more reason to feel privileged that he had invited her in.

'You work in the city?'

He nodded. 'I have an apartment in South Melbourne so not much commuting. Mostly just a tram ride along St. Kilda Road.'

'What sort of architect are you?'

'Basically residential.'

'What kind of projects?'

He grinned. 'Do you really have a wish for a long boring Saturday night?'

'That passionate, huh?'

'Eco-friendly homes or ones that use recycled or natural materials and less resources,' he said straight off with enthusiasm. 'And once it's built, it's energy efficient and doesn't suck the planet dry. I've done a lot of reading and research over recent years, made a lot of contacts, so I'm eager to get out into the world and see for myself what other like minds are doing.'

'Sounds exciting.' Jennifer tried to be positive even as her heart shrank a little at the reality of the knowledge that Sam would soon be gone from Bundilla, and her life. He had important work to do. She was only just getting to know him but instinctively felt she might eventually lose him. In contrast to shielding her heart, probably the wiser option, she decided to open it fully to Sam and show him how much she cared.

He continued, 'I want to check out adobe homes in the likes of Colorado and New Mexico that have a south orientation to the winter sun, with lots of windows to warm the house and solar panels for electricity off the grid. Basically, a green home using the earth's resources for free. They can still be functional and beautiful if people think outside the traditional concept of what a house should be. We need to open up our minds and think laterally these days when it comes to housing.'

Jennifer had finished her soup as he talked while his own bowl sat half empty and cooling.

'So, what about the aged care home planned for Bundilla? Any ideas on the drawing board yet? Do you intend incorporating your principles into that?'

He pulled a wry face. 'If I can convince the committee. I've already run some ideas by them but it means finding the right block of land in town facing north that's big enough for the whole complex to be built in a certain direction and to a certain end purpose.'

'Well, good luck with it. Bundilla desperately needs it. Small towns often have an aging population. People living alone, unable to take proper care of themselves, stretching home services, when they would be so much more comfortable in a proper nursing environment. But I imagine it must be hard to convince them how much better off they would be when they want to stay in their own home.'

'I agree. Grace apparently coped well until recently.'

'She was amazingly mobile and certainly seemed quite sprightly.'

'Some people age slowly and gracefully. She was one of them.'

A silence fell between them while Sam finished his soup and added another log to the fire.

'How much longer before you finish up here?' Jennifer looked around the room and rubbed her arms.

'Another few weekends maybe.' Sam shrugged. 'Then I'll only need to come back for occasional meetings about the new build.'

'Will that interfere with your travel plans?'

He shook his head. 'Nothing booked yet. That'll have to wait until I'm free. Besides investigating green homes being built all over the planet, I have another overseas stop on my schedule.' It sounded mysterious, but he didn't elaborate.

186

'You're going to be busy. I don't suppose you're considering returning for social visits?' she hinted without any subtlety whatsoever.

Sam threw back his head and laughed. 'I could at that,' he drawled. 'Hmm. Who do I know around here that's a big enough magnet?'

They moved away from the fire to settle on the sofa. He looked down at her sitting snuggled comfortably beside him, cosy and warm, invitation on her dreamy face and those luscious pink lips ripe for the taking. He cupped her face in his hands and drew her closer. To be lost in kissing again for a while seemed the most natural thing to do.

Much later, when they straightened their mussed hair and clothes, rumpled and flushed from deep kissing and some tentative physical exploration of each other sprawled out on the sofa, Sam ran a hand through his waves and grinned.

'Maybe we need coffee to sober up.'

'Who said I want to?' she teased so

he stole another slow kiss before reluctantly struggling to his feet.

While in the kitchen filling the kettle and setting it to boil on the Esse, Jennifer had stretched, risen and strolled over barefoot to join him. She hugged him from behind and wrapped her arms around his waist as he washed and dried their mugs and spooned in coffee.

'We never do seem to get around to talking about Grace,' Jennifer said. 'I'd love to know more about her.'

Sam turned around to face her, leaning against the bench and pulling her against him. 'Then, my dear Jennifer,' he kissed her nose and let out a long reflective sigh, 'you are about to be informed. Are you up for it?'

'Of course. But only if you want to share.' She held his gaze. 'I get the impression her story is going to be intriguing but possibly sad.'

Sam considered for a moment. 'More like unfortunate.' He reached out for her hand and drew her back across the room to the sofa again. When Jennifer was comfortably settled against him, he said, 'Turns out, since Grace and Peter Charlton were engaged — and perhaps in the uncertainly and urgency of war — they must have fully explored their love, because she became pregnant.'

'Really?'

She turned to Sam in surprise and was about to ask what had happened to Grace's baby, because everyone in town had assumed Grace was a spinster, but she decided to let him continue.

'A young couple obviously very much in love.' He shrugged. 'Not knowing from one day to the next what would happen with Peter away fighting in the jungles of Vietnam. Understandable. That was the real reason Grace came to Bundilla and confided her situation to Barbara, who then persuaded Mel to help her. Apparently her family disowned her.'

Jennifer moaned. 'That's so heartless and unchristian.'

'Even in the seventies, there was still

huge stigma attached to unwed mothers. Meanwhile . . . ' Sam hesitated. 'Mel and Barbara discovered they couldn't have children.'

Jennifer focused intently on Sam at this news, her mind leaping ahead to an incredibly unbelievable possibility.

'Grace decided she couldn't cope with the shame of her child growing up knowing it was born outside marriage, so she suggested adoption to Mel and Barbara and they agreed.'

Jennifer's gaze doubled. As Sam had revealed all the pieces of the puzzle, realisation slowly dawned. 'You're Grace and Peter's son!' she whispered reverently.

Sam nodded and his jaw ground as he controlled his emotions at the moment of truth.

'Oh, Sam.' Jennifer instinctively reached out and hugged him tight for a long while during which neither of them spoke at all. When she finally pulled away, she said, 'So in hospital on the night Grace died, you were saying goodbye to your mother, not an aunt at all?'

His eyes glittered stoically with unshed tears. Jennifer gently cupped his face and kissed him, seeing how vulnerable he had become at voicing the truth to someone while she absorbed everything he had just confided.

'Giving up the child of the man she loved must have been heartbreaking,' she said.

'Judging from their letters, Grace and Peter *did* share a great love. But I wonder that seeing me grow up all those years wasn't agony for her or some personal form of torture. Grace didn't want anyone to know I was her son. I'll never know why she didn't make that fateful decision. To punish herself for giving me up?'

'Do you blame her?' Jennifer probed tactfully.

Sam groaned and closed his eyes. 'Not really, I guess, but deep down I wish she'd had the courage to keep me.'

Jennifer slowly shook her head, still coming to terms with the breadth of information Sam had just shared. She understood now why Sam never called Mel and Barbara Mum and Dad. The cause of their split as a family? No matter who had raised Sam or who his natural parents were, all of them must be incredibly proud of the admirable man he had become.

Idly, Jennifer rolled the knowledge over in her mind that Sam was actually Sam Charlton. Because it was early days yet, no doubt he was still struggling with the issues and dynamics of it all. It would take time until he sorted it all out in his mind. Was that why he was going away? For time and space to let the reality of his life settle more comfortably on him?

'Eventually,' Sam was talking again so Jennifer once more gave him her attention. 'Grace intended to leave Bundilla but when it came down to it, she couldn't. She wanted to watch me grow up on the condition I never knew she was my mother until after she died.'

'It must have been agonizing for her.' Jennifer grasped Sam's hands firmly in her own. 'And you.' She frowned. 'Did you get to speak to Grace as your mother before she died?'

His anguished glance told her all she needed to know. 'She sent for me but had lapsed into unconsciousness before I arrived.'

'Maybe it was meant to be that way,' she offered. 'How did your parents — sorry, I mean, Mel and Barbara — how did they cope with having to reveal the truth?'

'Mel told me. Barbara couldn't. She's always hidden behind him. Mel's the stronger partner in their marriage. He wanted me to take over his company. Perhaps a reason even that he agreed to adopt me. I was a boy and he probably had my future all mapped out alongside him. But I refused. That was his choice, his life's success and interest, not mine.'

'Is that why your relationship is strained with them?'

'More or less,' he admitted. 'There's another matter, too, but I'm trying not to let it eat me up. It's going to take time to digest it all. To all intents and purposes the people that raise you *are* your parents, but I personally wish Grace had wanted me to know I was her son. All three adults lived with the secret for over thirty years.' Sam shrugged. 'It was her decision to make but I would have loved to know. I might have even been inclined to come back to Bundilla because she was here. Spent time with her. Changed my career path. Who knows what it might have meant for my life?'

'So that's why Mel transferred the cottage title over to you?'

'He virtually considered it was hers anyway. I found out they never charged her rent all those years. Mel the sharp businessman who never passes up the opportunity to make a dollar, totally backed down on that one. I respect him for that.' He paused. 'But not much else at the moment,' he muttered. 'Grace worked in the office at Mahoney's Emporium for years, apparently, and she had quite a tidy sum tucked away but she was on a pension later in life.'

With both of them still reeling from disclosures and revelations, they sat in silence for a while. Then Jennifer said, 'When it's all said and done, the family unit is so important. It's the backbone of society. To be treasured.'

'I agree,' he murmured.

Jennifer watched Sam, trying to imagine him coming to terms with his new life situation as the natural son of Grace Evans and Peter Charlton. Not surprisingly, he looked incredibly vulnerable and shaken. Weary. She understood now why he had been so grumpy that first morning they met in the cafe. He would have only just learned everything. She just wanted to draw him into her arms and hold him. Offer comfort. Let him know she was there for him always. And kisses, she thought with mischief. Lots of those, too.

When he glanced across at her, she saw the raw emotion he had suppressed in recent weeks. He just stared at her, lost.

'Sam?' she whispered. 'Come here.'

Next moment, she leaned back against the sofa and he sank against her, his body warm against hers. She breathed in his familiar male scent as his head rested against her shoulder and they snuggled together in what she anticipated would be nothing more than a caring embrace.

But he tilted up his face, his arms slid around her, moulding her tight and she lost her direction. His raised hand traced a gentle line down her face, then it cupped the back of her head and he drew her close. She read longing in his eyes. Perhaps reflected from hers? His mouth found hers and lingered. Soft. Unhurried. Good thing they were sitting down. Well, reclined really, or her knees might have given way again.

She gripped his T-shirt, closed her eyes and enjoyed the golden moment.

'I'm sure I should go,' she murmured when they drew apart.

'Stay,' he pleaded.

Jennifer caught the genuine edge of

need in his voice and guessed what he was suggesting. She could move away. End it now. But he was so close, and she adored him. Sam Keats was the kind of man you respected and trusted.

Jennifer considered her upbringing and hesitated over making a decision. She had no guarantees with Sam that their relationship would ever progress to a lifetime's commitment. It was early days between them and there were so many unknowns. Their attraction had developed swiftly and strong, catching them both by surprise given its unexpected force.

He would leave eventually, and every weekend he returned to Bundilla brought that fateful time closer. Predicting this, she wanted to know and share the full experience of loving, but only with this one special man. She would never contemplate it with anyone else. Her whole life, she had always assumed it would only come after the traditional route of a courtship and marriage. But times had changed and she saw no shame in genuine responsive love between a man and a woman.

Was this how Grace and Peter had felt, tugged by the threatening separation of war, demonstrating the depth of their love for each other?

Since meeting Sam Keats now, her emotions and gut instincts, pushed by her strong love for him, battled with her Christian upbringing. Until now, she had never needed to challenge that ideal. Should she wait until a husband one day placed a ring on her finger and made it legal? Or should she express her love for Sam in a way for which both of them yearned? She didn't contemplate for one moment that such a step between two people who genuinely loved each other was in any way tawdry, but would be a beautiful mutual expression of that love.

'So, you're going then?' Sam prompted, apprehension in his gaze, waiting for her decision.

Jennifer gave a mock scowl. 'I think that rain's getting heavier.'

He guessed the direction of her thoughts, grinned, and shrugged. 'No point getting soaked when you could stay dry here.'

'Makes sense to me.'

They smiled at each other, knowing they had crossed a line. His gaze reached into her soul, filling her with wild sweet longing.

'So, what now?' Sam murmured.

'Another kiss would be nice.'

He hesitated. 'So, we're just taking one day at a time?'

He sounded cautious like her, but Jennifer fully intended to savour every precious moment with him and see where it led. Then his hands moved over her, explored her, and she sighed with contentment. She definitely didn't want to be anywhere else.

After a while it seemed that the most natural next step was just a room away. Sam uncurled himself from beside her, removing his warmth, and she shivered. He gazed down upon her with such passion, took her hand and led her toward his bedroom.

'Are you sure?' He hesitated by the door.

She looked deeply into his warm brown eyes. 'My heart is in your hands.'

He dipped his head and kissed her in the hollow sensitive place of her neck. 'So's mine.'

He opened the door, led her inside and closed it behind them.

6

Early next morning, with the garden dripping and glistening, the rain-washed streets shiny and wet, Jennifer stood just inside the front door of Sam's cottage enfolded within his arms, enjoying being thoroughly kissed.

'You'll make me late for work,' she teased, breaking away but lingering because they had shared the most awesome night together.

But, with daylight, reality loomed and she needed to get back to the flat, shower and change, and head for the café.

'See you later for brunch, then,' he promised.

She stole one last kiss and forced herself to leave.

As she cycled in the refreshing chill, Jennifer realised she and Sam had, if anything, just complicated an already knotty relationship. She considered dashing in to David's early short service at

St. Luke's but was pushed for time. Besides, she wasn't sure she could sit in a church pew filled with so much love for Sam and face up to the guilt of tarnishing her religious beliefs. Yet when they shared something so beautiful and right, it didn't even enter Jennifer's radar that the night she and Sam had spent together was in any way inappropriate. She and Sam were two mature and sensible people who had made a decision based on genuine love. It was the future that troubled her now, not what they had done.

In the flat, Rose shuffled about the kitchen in robe and slippers cooking eggs and bacon.

'Morning, dear.' She turned her cheek for her daughter's kiss.

Jennifer hugged her mother and pinched pieces of bacon and toast. 'Morning. Thanks for understanding and not judging me,' she said frankly.

'I know whatever you do, Jennifer, is with an honest heart. Just be sure of your feelings, dear.'

'I am,' she promised. 'Rachel up?'

Rose shook her head.

As it happened, the day's unpredictable spring weather flummoxed everyone when the overnight storm was banished and the sun burst out from behind thinning clouds to draw out townsfolk and sightseers alike.

The café was crowded. All day, Jennifer and the emergency waitress called in to help shared the busy load barely managing their designated breaks. Sam's arrival mid-morning was a potentially tantalising distraction, but Jennifer was caught up across the room with no hope of weaving her way back to speak to him. Olivia served him and they barely exchanged more than a distant longing glance.

Jennifer scooted between tables, delivering orders, and eventually stole a few moments to target Sam's table. 'I'll be tied up here until late,' she complained.

'I have to head back to the city early this afternoon,' he replied.

Jennifer frowned and shook her head,

lowering her voice. 'I can't possibly get away.'

They swapped wry grins and he left before she had a chance to talk to him again. Later he returned and, in the middle of the café, sought her out and gave her a warm meaningful kiss in view of everyone. Receiving interested stares, Jennifer thought *It's out now* and sighed, uttering hurried murmured goodbyes between customers and waving as he left. No time to dwell on how lonely her heart would be all week, for she was immediately plunged back into the busy demands of table service, making coffee and bearing armloads of dirty dishes into the kitchen.

* * *

From cloud nine, Jennifer was soon abruptly brought back to earth with a thud of reality and her focus snatched from Sam. On welfare day Jennifer approached Rachel, believing if she caught her immediately she should still have money left, but her sister only offered a token amount.

'This is not what we agreed, Rachel,' Jennifer said, exasperated.

'You decided the amount. I didn't.'

'I worked out all our rental and living expenses and that is *not* your one-quarter share. Mother's on a pension but she contributes.'

'Well, that's all you're getting. If it's not enough, too bad.'

'Too bad for you,' Jennifer advised sternly. 'I need the rest by the end of the day. Rent's due Friday. You're perfectly fit and healthy to work. You're just too lazy to bother. Mum and Dad didn't raise us to rely on welfare.'

'Mum does.'

'She's over 65 and too old to work anymore. Besides, you know she's not capable. She raised a family of five and worked hard all her life alongside our father in the church.' Jennifer lowered her voice. 'I need the shortfall, Rachel. I've covered for you in the past but I can't do it anymore.'

Her sibling glared. 'Well I don't have it.'

'I could get you a job in Sue's café.'

'I'm not serving cups of tea to old ladies,' she replied in horror.

'Then what do you want to do?' Jennifer sighed and laid a hand gently on her arm, more than prepared to listen and see if she could help.

Rachel roughly shrugged her off. For a moment, a look of such deep unhappiness clouded her face, Jennifer thought she might finally break and confide. But a determined hardness took over again, a fake front. Glaring, pretending to be brave, Rachel said sharply, 'I'm not putting up with your nagging anymore. I'm leaving.'

Jennifer grew cold and froze at her announcement. She was about to blast out a retort until she recalled David's words. So she stopped herself, took a deep breath and asked calmly, 'Are you sure? Where on earth will you go?'

'We don't know yet. We're just going away,' she delivered a smug teaser.

The *we* made Jennifer's heart sink, but she hid her distress at the unwelcome news even while her stomach churned with worry. Boomer was the worst influence.

'I'll be glad to get out of this backwater town. There's nothing here.' Rachel stormed off to her room.

Feeling helpless, Jennifer followed. 'Do you have any plans?'

Rachel snatched up her clothes from cupboards and drawers and stuffed them into a large backpack. 'Of course not. We're going wherever the road takes us.'

'Will you keep in touch? Let your mother and I know where you are?'

'Yeah. Right. Like you care about me,' she blurted out miserably.

Rose had been hovering in the background silently, witnessing the conversation. Now she stepped forward and faced her confused youngest child.

'I know you're hurting, Rachel,' she said calmly. 'And I wish you would stay, but I'll always be here for you. You'll be in my prayers.'

'Fat lot of good that will do.'

'It means we care and we'll be thinking of you,' Jennifer reminded her, wrapping an arm about her mother's shoulder.

This sudden whirlwind departure was far from impulsive. Jennifer guessed it had been planned for some time. So for the mother and sister left behind, the wrench of separation was acute. Rachel, however, had longer to grow accustomed to an escape that had always been inevitable.

On impulse, Jennifer grabbed her sister in a fierce hug. Rachel hurled herself away, trying to show she didn't care, but deep down Jennifer just hoped she felt an equal sense of loss. Rose had accepted the decision with quiet composure.

'Do you have everything?' Jennifer asked carefully.

'I have nothing,' she yelled with painful honesty as she backed away.

Stoic until then, Rose sank against Jennifer at the heartbreaking outburst.

'Your choice,' Jennifer challenged quietly, clutching at hope. 'You can still stay.'

'I'm not being smothered here anymore.'

They endured Rachel's thunderous black glare. Their stalemate was interrupted by the roaring note of Boomer's motorbike rumbling down the street. Jennifer gulped back dread and panic for her sister.

She watched Rachel strap her pack onto the bike, pull on a helmet, climb up behind Boomer, and hug him tight as they sped away. Jennifer and her mother stood for a long moment in the silence, holding each other up.

'Let's go get dinner,' Jennifer suggested, although she doubted either of them had any appetite.

* * *

In the following weeks, they heard nothing of Rachel and had no idea where she might be. Incredibly, the flat seemed lonely without her spirited insolence. With warmer weather settling in, Rose occupied her time with gardening and Jennifer plunged herself even deeper into work. Her mother was already picking the first of the summer vegetable crop and the manse garden burst into a glorious display with her namesake roses.

Jennifer's life with Sam became a juggle of grabbing moments when they could be together. Her heart and mind were so completely absorbed by her love for him that with a huge effort she pushed the future away to the back of her mind without consideration.

Too soon, Grace's cottage was empty except for the solitary mattress on the bedroom floor. The estate affairs were settled and Sam's job done. The few treasures and valuable keepsakes remaining, he securely stowed in a small heavy safe in a corner of a bedroom. Jennifer considered it rather sad that a person's life could be reduced to such a small repository. All of Grace's photos, diaries, letters from Peter and other papers Sam considered important, he took back to his Melbourne apartment.

In the light of his confidences and revelations, Jennifer no longer gave any heart or consideration to buying the cottage. It meant too much to him, and with Rachel gone the flat felt roomier, so she accepted that her sharing days with her mother would continue.

Sam regularly phoned from Melbourne but his visits to Bundilla were reduced to fortnightly. Jennifer sensed the writing on the wall. Her heart and mind turned grey, for she had fallen deeply in love. He didn't invite her to the city and pride wouldn't let her beg or ask. She thought she meant more to him than portrayed from his indifferent attitude to her these days. A cruel blast of reality she could have done without. But, on the other hand, Sam had made no promises and they had agreed to take one day at a time. She had just always hoped that the time would never end.

Good thing the hectic summer tourist season was in full swing in town, spilling over into the café. It kept her mind occupied, but her heart discouraged over Sam's lack of involvement in her life and what Jennifer had thought a blossoming relationship. She had not entrusted her love to him lightly, nor given her heart away to any man before, so she was ignorant of the approach she should take in the situation.

Jennifer was also plagued with the added emotional stress of Rachel's continued absence, Christmas having come and gone without her. The only bright spot was a few days when two of her brothers, Luke from Adelaide and Joshua from nearby Castlemaine, each separately made the pilgrimage back to Bundilla to spend time with their family. Both were horrified of course at Rachel's defiant disappearance.

Then, one rare and wonderful weekend when Sam returned to Bundilla for an architectural consultation, his mood was tense and excited.

'The new Bundilla aged care complex is humming along and groundwork should begin later in the year,' he announced as they walked hand-in-hand through the leafy fruit-laden orchard behind the cottage — private, able to talk, making use of the glorious summer days. 'I've arranged for my partner to oversee the project,' he said cautiously.

A rush of alarm flashed through Jennifer's chest. Did that mean he wasn't returning anymore? She gaped at him, waiting for an explanation, trying not to appear too besotted in case her heart was about to be crushed. Time stopped until he spoke. The bombshell landed soon enough.

'I'm going overseas to America, the south and western states like Colorado and New Mexico, to investigate adobe-built green and solar homes.'

As his magnetic brown eyes shone and his dreamy lips spread into an engaging smile, Jennifer knew that, in his elation, Sam had completely missed her air of desolation. But how could he see something that she only felt in her heart?

'Australia has similar climate zones to those areas and the potential for home designs based on passive solar principles and using solar panels for off-the-grid power generation are enormous.'

His passion was infectious, the exhilaration on his face unmistakeable. He'd spoken of this before. His dream research. Jennifer's spirit shrivelled like paper in flames. She'd heard of loving and letting go. A saintly sentiment maybe, but it sucked. And hurt like mad when it hit. She dragged up enthusiasm for him from a pit someplace deep in her soul. Forced herself to be charitable, and smiled.

'That's wonderful. You've made definite plans, then?' Without consulting me, a tiny voice nagged. Therefore how important am I in your life? It was painful to realise that at that distance, on another continent, their connection would be even weaker. Anchored in Bundilla as she had chosen to be, America might as well be another planet. Sam gave her the dates. Only weeks away!

Then he stunned her with his next comment. 'I'd love you to come with me,' he said so quietly, she wondered if she had misheard. By the look of anticipation on Sam's face, he was assuming her reply would be fast, positive and automatic.

What a tempting invitation — but no clue what it meant for their relationship. Would they just travel together? See the world? She didn't even have a passport. Jennifer was torn between staying where she finally felt settled, or taking a leap of faith to join Sam. Who knew where they would end up?

She felt so helpless. Knowing all along that this time would come did not make the decision any easier now that the moment had finally arrived. It was such a huge request, Jennifer couldn't even begin to answer. She always planned. Snap decisions weren't usually on her radar.

'How long will you be away?'

'Could be months. A year.'

'Are you ever coming back?'

'I'm not leaving you, Jennifer. I'm asking you to join me,' he pointed out in response to her accusing tone.

'Sam,' she hedged, 'my mother is just becoming settled. I need to know she's safe and okay. I don't know how long that will take but I can see positive changes happening for her. She's not yet at a stage where I would feel comfortable leaving her alone. And since Rachel's disappeared, I want to be here in case she returns.'

'Rose will still be here if that happens,' he pointed out.

'I know but ... I'm finding it a difficult choice.'

'Is it?' Sam challenged, clearly hurt by her hesitation. 'Everything will still be here when you get back. Life's a moving target, Jennifer. It doesn't stand still or stay the same forever. It's always changing. I need to do this,' he argued.

Jennifer could see this was not a decision or choice to be equally decided. Sam had already made his. With or without her, he was leaving.

'I can't,' she whispered.

'Come with me,' he pleaded, catching up her hands and pulling her close, driving her to distraction and the edge of an emotional cliff.

She slowly shook her head.

'Then you've just broken my heart.'

Their hands slid apart. 'Ditto,' Jennifer said miserably.

A long wretched silence hung between them.

'I thought you'd come with me. Don't you want us to be together?' Sam accused.

'Of course I do,' she said desperately. 'I've just explained why not.'

'That's it, then?' Sam said desolately.

She shook off her sense of guilt. 'Seems like it.' They stared at each other blankly like strangers. 'Will you keep in touch?' she asked in a small voice.

Sam shrugged. 'I'll try. I'll be on the move most of the time.'

He was so noncommittal that Jennifer almost felt offended. In explanation, she said, 'I've never been adventurous. It was bad enough having to move

217

house every few years and make new friends.'

'Unless you get out into the big wide world, you'll never know that you have the strength and what it has to offer. Please reconsider, Jen. Come with me,' he begged again.

Tugged between her dream and her love, it should have been an easy choice. Jennifer moaned. 'You're cruel, Sam Keats — '

'Charlton,' he said suddenly. 'I'm taking my father's name.'

'Oh.' His fierce retort took Jennifer by surprise. 'That's nice.' She wondered how Mel and Barbara would feel about that news.

'I can't persuade you to change your mind?'

'Sam — '

'It's okay. I don't understand, but I accept your decision.'

They stood eyeing each other bleakly again, a wasteland of limbo stretching out between them. Both filled with the wrenching pain of wanting to be together, but circumstances pulling their lives in opposite directions.

Sam broke away, hands on hips, and paced. 'I'm going to America on the journey to making my dream come true. Maybe I can help with yours.'

Jennifer frowned, puzzled.

'I have a proposal to make.' He eyed her with such loving mischief, Jennifer's heart skipped a beat. Surely he wasn't going to ask her *that*?

'I'm making Grace's cottage available for sale.' He paused. 'If you still want to buy.'

A stunned Jennifer didn't know whether to laugh or cry. Laugh with the ridiculous irony of finally being given the opportunity of achieving her family's dream, or cry because by accepting Sam's offer, it sealed the fact of going their separate ways. For how long? Forever? Was this the end?

Jennifer dithered. If she went off with Sam, she would be drifting. Rootless. Forsaking Rose and the home and stability she had craved much of her life. Absent if Rachel returned.

Unable to process his unbelievable offer, but afraid to accept it just yet, she stalled. 'I thought you wanted to keep it?'

'Originally, that was my thinking,' he admitted, 'But I've moved on. I've let go.' He eyed her steadily. 'I believe Rose needs it more.'

In that moment when their gaze met, Jennifer knew that Sam was giving up as much as she. Tears pooled in her eyes, threatening to spill over. With a hand over her mouth and lips trembling, she whispered, 'You'd really sell?'

Husky voice and clenched jaw. 'Strictly business.'

'Of course. Absolutely,' she said quickly, realising from his controlled emotions that this transaction was as staggering for him to overcome as it was for her. Sam was relinquishing his mother's home, but he would always hold and cherish his memories. They would be part of him wherever he went every day of his life.

'Deal?' he held out his hand.

Overwhelmed by this sudden momentous event in her life, Jennifer took it and nodded. She smiled through her tears. 'We haven't even discussed a figure.'

Sam shrugged. 'Market price?'

'Sure.'

Jennifer appreciated that Sam had given up his dearest possession and offered custody of it to Jennifer for Rose. For neither of them was it about the money. Sam didn't need it and Jennifer knew she could afford it now, based on assessment of her finances and the small but helpful government assistance she was entitled to receive toward the deposit. She had two jobs. She would easily cope with a mortgage. *But what about your own life?* a tiny niggling voice whispered at the back of her mind.

★　★　★

Days later in Stewart Dalton's office, Sam and Jennifer signed the Transfer of Land contracts and associated legal

221

papers. Although it would take some weeks for the title deed to be officially changed over, Sam dangled the front door keys in front of her as he had suggested she take immediate vacant possession.

For Jennifer the moment was bitter sweet, of course. Now the decision was made, Sam appeared anxious to leave. She knew his car was packed and he would head back home to Melbourne as soon as he walked out the door.

And she could now haunt Mr. Wilson's shop to start filling their new home with treasured old furniture pieces. An empty victory, perhaps?

When Jennifer reached out and took the keys, Sam folded his hands over hers. 'I hope you and Rose know much happiness there. It's time Grace's cottage had more life and laughter inside its walls.'

'Thank you.' She reached out and hugged him, closing her eyes and breathing in his warmth and familiar smell, making the moment last. 'We'll take good care of it.'

Standing to one side, Stewart Dalton looked on with interest. Jennifer ached at such a public farewell and filled with hollow dread that, after today, he would no longer be in her life. If they had taken leave of each other in private, she might have thrown in everything and begged him to take her with him.

Jennifer noticed Stewart had discreetly disappeared from his office and closed the door, leaving them alone together. Sam produced a wrapped parcel from his briefcase and handed it to her.

'What's this?'

'A keepsake.'

Intrigued, she opened it to reveal twin framed photographs of his parents: the lovely picture of a younger Grace and Peter in army uniform probably taken before leaving for Vietnam.

'I like to think they'll be here watching over you,' he murmured.

'I'll probably always think of the cottage as belonging to Grace,' Jennifer confessed. She had lived so long and quietly in the house with the memory of Peter sitting gently on her shoulder. Her spirit would linger forever.

'I don't do long goodbyes,' Sam admitted, locking his briefcase and looking awkward. 'Never been good at it.'

For a heartbeat they stood apart, and she held her breath until Sam groaned and squeezed her tight in a crushing hug, burrowing his face into her hair. He drew away and tenderly kissed her forehead, then ran a finger around her lips before dipping his mouth to hers in a long and passionate kiss. It filled her soul like an intoxicating drug, meant to last them both until they met again. Perhaps.

Then he was gone and Jennifer stood alone with her doubts in Stewart's office. This brutal parting must have been what Grace felt a long time ago when Peter went to war. She now fully understood and sympathised with her emptiness on separation.

That evening after work, Jennifer returned to her mother at the flat, a complete wreck, missing a sense of purpose, her misery tinged with the unbelievable joy and gift she could give her mother.

'So he's gone then?' Rose said as she walked in. Filled with desolation, Jennifer just nodded. 'Will you hear from him again?'

'I hope so, but apparently he'll be moving around a lot.'

'I thought you two were — ' Perceptive Rose paused, choosing her next words carefully. 'Close friends.'

'We were. Are. Very good friends.' Jennifer found it heartbreaking to admit, for she had given up the chance to be with him for her mother.

Rose persisted. 'You both seemed to have such a strong connection.'

'Yes, we did.' Another vast understatement, bordering on a lie.

'He was such a gentleman.' Rose's mind was sharper these days and Jennifer suspected she was reflecting on her husband. 'So polite and good-looking.'

Oh, rub it in, Jennifer thought morosely, filled with self-pity, although she was reaping the poor harvest of her own impossible decision. Had she been foolish to turn her back on the one special person to enter her life? *Who had pleaded with her to go with him?*

'Yes, he was,' she finally agreed.

How could she not? Sam Keats — no, Charlton — was all those things and far more to her than she would ever admit to anyone. And she had let him go.

Fed up with sinking into regret and life without Sam — how deeply she missed him already — Jennifer shook herself to get a grip to embrace the thrill of breaking the exciting news to her mother.

'I have a surprise for you.'

With great fanfare, Jennifer blindfolded Rose, who played along. Arm-in-arm, they took the mysterious five-minute walk to the unknown destination in silence. Jennifer felt her mother's sense of expectation and calm, knowing she didn't have a clue what would be revealed.

Finally they came to a halt and

Jennifer untied the scarf blindfold. As it slid from her mother's eyes, they stood in front of a familiar white picket fence.

'What are we doing at Grace Evans' cottage?'

'Welcome to your new home.' Rose turned and frowned at her daughter, speechless. 'It's ours. I bought it.'

As she stood gaping, tears slowly trickled down her mother's cheeks. 'It's really ours?' she whispered, incredulous. Jennifer nodded. 'But how on earth did you manage it?'

She reached out for her mother's hand. 'Besides my own savings and a government grant, remember now and again you gave me small amounts of your leftover pension to invest for a rainy day? Well,' Jennifer beamed, indicating the cottage with a flourish. 'This is our rainy day.'

Rose pressed her free hand over her mouth and shook her head.

Concerned that she might have done the wrong thing, Jennifer clarified, 'You don't mind that I — '

'Good heavens, no, dear. You're a wonderful unselfish daughter. I love you dearly. How do I ever thank you?'

'You don't. Family don't expect thanks. I would do anything for you, Mum. Just be happy here, okay? You deserve it.'

Jennifer linked an arm with her mother and they stood staring at the cottage for a long while. Eventually, she suggested, 'Shall we go check out our new home?'

Although still in awe, shaking her head in disbelief, Jennifer smiled to herself when Rose's eyes immediately started roaming over the rambling neglected garden.

Reading her mind, Jennifer chuckled. 'There's more. Wait until you see the orchard out the back.'

'Really?' Her mother chuckled with the first sign of genuine heart, reminiscent of the woman she had been in Jennifer's childhood. Jennifer turned the front door key and both women stepped across the threshold into the start of their new future together.

Every spare minute after work during the week at the legal office, and on weekends at the café, Jennifer renovated the cottage. Because she was younger and more physically able, she cleaned every corner of every room from top to bottom, scrubbed down and prepared all the walls for painting. Rose disappeared into the garden for hours: trimming, weeding, carting in wheelbarrow loads of manure, and mulching hay.

It gave Jennifer much delight to bring home heritage paint colours to choose, allowing her mother to make most decisions. After all, this was really *her* home. Unfortunately, the lonely evening hours gave Jennifer too much time to think of Sam. She missed him dearly. She loved Grace's cottage and her mother, but she soon came to realise that she loved Sam more. She should not have been surprised that he became more dear to her with every single day apart.

Her love had not diminished but grown, her ache like a painful illness.

From time to time in her own private dilemma, Jennifer ran her thumb over the photographs of Grace and Peter and sighed, pleading with them for guidance. 'What would you two have done?'

Should she have grabbed the opportunity after all? But that would have meant abandoning her mother and, at the time, she didn't want to risk a relapse in her mother's recovery. In the weeks since Sam's departure, the improvement in Rose's health was like a minor miracle. And she was certainly due for one of those in her life. Colour flushed her cheeks. An animated smile and happy contented weariness filled her expression at the end of each day.

Once Rose, too, glanced across at the photograph and commented pointedly to her daughter, 'How fortunate to have truly loved if only for a brief time.'

Jennifer knew the hint was aimed squarely at her relationship with Sam.

Being in the cottage brought back warm memories of their brief time together. On weekdays when she could, she finished early and cycled down to the mobile library van to use its internet connection. Short emails at least let her know where he was in America.

Then on one momentous day, Jennifer and Rose, helped with John Parker's ute and trailer, moved their humble possessions into Grace's cottage. Jennifer proudly returned their flat key to him and the new phase of their life began.

Not long after, matters were shaken up for everyone with a single unexpected telephone call. Jennifer nearly dropped the handset when she heard Rachel's voice. She beckoned madly to her mother and pressed the loudspeaker button so they could both hear the conversation.

'Rachel, it's so good to hear from you.'

She refrained from blurting out *Thank God you're still alive*. It had been months since she left and they had despaired of hearing anything.

'I just wanted to let you and Mum know I'm all right.'

'Thank you. We appreciate it.' Jennifer paused. 'Where are you?'

'Up on the northern New South Wales coast.'

Jennifer squashed her surprise but trod carefully with her responses. 'You've certainly travelled a long way. I bet it's lovely up there near the beach.'

'I guess so.'

When the line went silent for a moment, Jennifer listened to her sisterly instincts and ventured brightly, 'So, everything okay with you?'

'Um . . . Boomer dumped me and took off last week.'

'Oh.' She exchanged a worried glance with her mother. Rachel was alone and far from home. Patience, Jennifer, she told herself. She was an adult. Don't coddle.

'We had a big argument,' she told them reluctantly.

'I'm sorry to hear that.'

'Don't be.'

'So, what's that going to mean for you?' Jennifer gently asked.

'Huh,' Rachel said wryly, 'I've realised he was a huge jerk and I'm well done with him. I didn't like where he wanted to go and what he wanted to do. Don't ask,' she added quickly. 'He's gone now.'

'Okay. So, what are your plans?'

'Not sure. Don't have any at the moment.'

'Are you thinking to stay up there or come back to Bundilla? I could send the bus fare — '

'No,' Rachel replied with swift certainty. 'Actually, I've got a job.'

Rose and Jennifer beamed at each other. 'Great. So you're staying a while?'

'Yeah. Over the summer at least. It's the busy tourist season and there's heaps of work up here. Been thinking about it a bit, but I might kind of work my way back.'

Jennifer gave her mother a silent

thumbs up. 'Well, keep in touch, sis, when you can, okay?'

'Yeah.' A short pause. 'Thanks.'

'You know we're always here for you.'

'I know.' A note of wry tolerance filtered into Rachel's voice.

Jennifer's heart burst to think her little sister might just have learnt the first of many life lessons the hard way. She sent up yet another silent prayer, one of many to higher powers recently, grateful for her sister's safety.

Before she hung up, Rachel asked, 'So, what's happening in town?'

'Funny you should ask.' Jennifer told her about buying Grace's cottage.

'No way!'

'Eat your words, little sister,' she teased fondly.

They chatted until Rachel declared she was in a public phone box and her coins had run out.

That night, Jennifer was aware that Rose watched her more closely than usual.

'So nice to hear Rachel is out in the

world growing independent and doing what she wants,' her mother said. 'Even if it may not have been our choice.'

'Yes, it is really.' There was a loaded pause during which Jennifer sensed what was coming next.

'I do hope that you will follow your own dreams and your own heart in life, too,' she stressed.

Jennifer glanced across at her calm and wise and perceptive mother, struck with the sudden truth that she had not been so ignorant after all as to what her oldest daughter had sacrificed.

'Remember Grace Evans, dear. She was not to know how brief her happiness would be, but she took the chance anyway and loved a man with all her heart, risking scandal and shame. There are no guarantees in life for any of us, dear. Grasp every day and live it.'

Stunned by her mother's quiet subtle advice, all Jennifer could say was, 'I'll be fine.'

Rose frowned. 'Will you, dear?'

Jennifer's mind screamed out *No!*

and she regarded her mother's hint with honest deep thought for her own life and future. How liberating to no longer feel obligated to anyone else, for she knew that was exactly what her mother was suggesting. Rose was recovered. Rachel, finally, was making her own way. Her brothers were off living their own lives.

Was this the break she always hoped to make one day? But this soon? Today? How vast the repercussions of Rachel's telephone call. If only her little sister knew what she had innocently unleashed.

Jennifer's heart was no longer here. Hadn't been since Sam left. Not really. She glanced around the cottage. Comfortable, simply furnished complements — most of Mr. Wilson's treasures, and her own hard work.

Blessing her mother's timely unassuming insight, and knowing what it would mean for both of them, Jennifer asked softly, 'Are you sure?'

Rose smiled gently. 'Don't even ask, dear.'

7

Jennifer's first step the very next morning was to cycle madly down to the post office and apply for her passport. That this took weeks did nothing for her impatience. Harder still was having to tell both Stewart and Sue, her two wonderful employers, that she wanted an indefinite leave of absence. When told why, they almost pushed her out their respective doors.

Stewart just gave her a gentle knowing smile and wished her well. 'I'll watch out for Rose,' he promised.

Sue flung her hands in the air, laughed and said, 'Well, I guess it had to happen eventually. And Sam Keats of all people. Who would have thought?'

Jennifer didn't correct her that it was now Sam Charlton. He had held the knowledge of his birth identity close. They would all find out eventually.

She had lots of sick pay and holiday leave due to her, rarely having taken a day off; so after allowing for her flights, she squirreled away most of her money to keep up her cottage payments, planning to travel on a shoestring budget. Generous Sam might have other ideas, but she was prepared and determined to contribute her share toward costs.

Only when all arrangements were in place, and Jennifer finally had the official passport document in her hand, did she make a move to locate Sam. Yes, she would go to him; but no, she would not tell him she was coming. First she had to find him.

Logically, she phoned his Melbourne office. When she introduced herself, it surprised and gratified her to realise that the staff knew exactly who she was. Knowing Sam and how he held things close to his heart, she warmed to think he may have mentioned her existence to his co-workers. Therefore it was a breeze to acquire his last known address: a hotel in Albuquerque, New Mexico, where he was researching adobe houses and planned to remain for at least another four to seven days.

'I can give you the address,' his assistant offered.

'That would be great.' Jennifer tucked the phone into her shoulder and rummaged about the kitchen for a scrap of paper and a pen. Never handy when you needed them in a hurry. Thanking them profusely, she rang off, took a deep breath and told her mother she must leave immediately in order to catch him before he moved on again.

If letting Sam go had been difficult, taking leave of her mother and friends in Bundilla was heart-wrenching because she had no idea when she would be home again, nor what to expect at the other end when she arrived. Hopefully, two strong and warm open arms of welcome, for it would be freezing in the northern hemisphere.

She thought hauling her luggage, boarding the plane and taking off into the sky for the first time would be daunting and lonely, until she realised every other person in the world was doing the same, and it seemed to be the most natural thing these days to jump on a flight for somewhere else.

For her, it meant a fourteen-hour direct flight from Melbourne East and high above the vast Pacific Ocean into Los Angeles. Weary and nervous, she managed to grab a few hours' sleep before changing to a domestic leg of just over an hour into New Mexico. She took the shuttle service direct to his Parq Central hotel right on Central Avenue in the heart of the city, an historic urban oasis. A sumptuous cosy boutique hotel.

Reception informed her that Mr. Charlton was out for the day but usually returned for dinner. Exhausted, she almost fell asleep on one of the comfortable padded lobby sofas waiting for his return. Her stomach churned with excitement. She didn't want to doze off and miss his arrival, so she ordered endless coffees and paced back and forth near the lit fireplace in order to stay awake.

She needed to see his reaction when he first caught sight of her, and see him walk toward her. Would he still feel the same way? Still care? She'd taken a big risk coming all this way. Had she made a big mistake arriving unannounced from the desperate need for him in her heart?

After an eternity of expectation, when Sam finally entered the lobby, his dear and familiar face rosy-cheeked from the cold, his tall body wrapped up well in a black coat and thick scarf against the winter, she held her breath. For a disappointing moment, she thought he would stride right past, but an instinctual sideways glance flung casually in her direction brought him to a stop.

The heart-stopping second, when their eyes met and they smiled at each other, brought out Jennifer's checked emotions and tears filled her eyes. Her feet wouldn't move, but that didn't matter because Sam was hurling himself toward her. She did manage one step before his arms enveloped her and she was wrapped in a crushing hug.

'Boy are you the best sight in the universe.' His voice was muffled against her neck. He pulled back and shook his head, grinning. 'Nice surprise. I'm blown away.'

'That's a relief. Kiss me.'

He obliged, pulling her back into his embrace, his passion and her response a remedy healing her lonely ache of separation. His arms gripped tight around her waist and she slid her own up around his neck, dragging him close, prolonging the crushing kiss. The kind she had sorely missed. That left her in no doubt of his feelings.

He kept tasting her lips in thrilling teasing little bites. 'I'd love to take this further,' she admitted when she managed to break away, stifling a yawn, 'but I'm desperate for sleep. Tell me you have a huge sumptuous bed I can borrow for a while.'

'Of course.' He shook his head and frowned in distraction, as if clearing his mind of whatever had preoccupied it moments before; it seemed as if it hadn't actually sunk in yet that she was here and standing nervously in front of him.

'Anything I have is yours,' he murmured.

He picked up her bags, slid an arm possessively around her and led her away. Jennifer rested her head on his shoulder and snuggled into him as they rode up in the lift to the fourth floor. His key card let them into a modern room with historic charm, a stylish soothing retreat from the constant movement and bustle of Jennifer's last twenty-four hours.

She moved toward the window. 'Great view downtown.'

He wrapped his arms about her from behind and rested his chin on her shoulder. 'Mmm.'

She closed her eyes and felt his voice reverberate against her. Then she felt herself scooped up and deposited gently on the bed. She curled over onto her side as her shoes were removed and remembered nothing else before falling into a deep restorative sleep.

It was dark when she woke. A lamp shed soft light from a bedside table and since the curtains weren't drawn, she noticed stars twinkling outside. Jennifer struggled to sit up, feeling revived and watching Sam with his head bent over a laptop, its lit screen casting a glow across his face.

Hearing her movement, he glanced across at her and smiled. 'Hey, Sleeping Beauty.'

She pushed a hand through her tangle of long hair. 'Is it too late for dinner? I'm starving.'

'We can head on up to the Apothecary Lounge. It's a rooftop bar with an awesome view.'

'I must improve my appearance first,' she moaned. 'I must look a fright.'

'Never more gorgeous,' he chuckled, leaning over her and planting a light lingering kiss on her mouth.

'White lies are good.'

Jennifer discovered a rainfall shower in the gleaming white bathroom, then rummaged through her case to find a smart casual outfit and chose her best jeans paired with a soft jumper. She clipped on dangly earrings and slipped her feet into her only pair of low heels. Sam had changed, too, from his outdoor clothes into black slacks and a stylish top that clung to his every masculine muscle.

Jennifer grabbed a handful of the soft material and murmured seductively, 'If I still have an appetite later, I just might eat you for dessert.'

Sam pulled a tight restrained smile. 'Have to be a quick meal I'm afraid, because I still have more to do tonight.'

Jennifer suffered the rebuff graciously. 'Then I'll enjoy you while I can.'

Did he consider her pushy and clingy for chasing him across the world without an invitation? She had hardly expected to be swept off her feet, but she had anticipated something warmer. She smiled to hide her doubts, reassured when Sam's arm slid around her waist and he ushered her toward the door. She sighed. That was the Sam she remembered, warm and comforting beside her.

In the rooftop lounge, they ordered cocktails, then Sam opted for beef sliders from the tapas menu, and Jennifer chose the crispy calamari.

'I love this hotel,' Jennifer said, looking around. 'It's small and cosy, lots of atmosphere.'

'The Santa Fe railroad built this place in the 1920s as a hospital for its employees,' Sam explained in between hastily demolishing his burger.

'Hard to imagine, but I can see where they've kept the character of the original building.'

'So, tell me, how did this surprise visit come about?'

While they ate and drank, Jennifer was finally able to update Sam on what had happened in her life since he left. The amazing contact from Rachel and positive hope for her future. Rose's progress back to the gentle confident woman she used to be.

'She did rather give me a nudge to come find you,' Jennifer admitted sheepishly. When Sam just offered a vague smile, she chattered to cover the awkward silence. 'You wouldn't believe the improvement in Mother. Once we moved into Grace's cottage, it happened so swiftly. She changed almost overnight. It was such a relief to see life coming back into her face. And you wait until you see the garden.' Jennifer shook her head. 'When I left it was still magnificent.'

'Jen,' Sam began guardedly. 'I still need to research more homes while I'm here. I'll need at least two more days here if you can brave drives out into the country with me to see them. I've already set up appointments with agents and owners to view them.'

'Of course.'

'Sure you wouldn't rather take advantage of the shops?'

'When I haven't been with you for

months? Not likely. Unless I'd be in the way?'

'No,' he replied hastily, 'But after New Mexico, there are some properties up in Colorado I want to check out, too. You won't mind? You won't be bored?' Sounded awfully like he was trying to discourage her.

'I'm beginning to understand the depth of your passion,' she teased, sighing inside that it wasn't quite so important for her. 'It will be exciting to see the concept of people's green homes and how they work.'

'It's going to be chilly,' Sam warned.

Jennifer shrugged and edged closer. 'Well, it is winter. We can keep each other warm. Besides,' she added, 'I didn't come here to interrupt your trip. Just to let you know how much you mean to me.'

'Okay, that's settled.'

Jennifer knew this was a work trip for Sam but hadn't expected him to be quite so busy. She rejected her unease that he hadn't been more enthusiastic about her arrival. Wherever Sam was in the world, as long as she was with him, it didn't matter.

Then he talked about his plans for introducing more architectural designs into his business. 'I like to think I'm helping the world, one house at a time.' His eyes gleamed with possibility and eagerness, and he was sharing his dreams with her. 'Who said one person can't make a difference.'

She didn't brood over the fact that the state of the future between them still lay unspoken and unresolved. They were together; he was confiding his visions and dreams. That was enough, she convinced herself.

Sam turned serious. 'You certainly make a difference in my life,' he confided.

'I missed you after you left.'

Sam just flashed a warm returning smile but didn't echo or voice his own feelings. A pinch of anxiety unfurled in her stomach and niggled at the back of her mind. She gave herself a good mental shake and dismissed her insecurity. He obviously had other things on his mind. Jennifer thought the warm message in her eyes would have conveyed his desirability for her but when they returned to his room, he went straight back to work on his laptop, leaving her disappointed and flipping distractedly through the television channels. Eventually, yawning and still jetlagged, she changed and went to bed.

Next morning, she woke to find Sam's side of the bed unslept in.

'I didn't want to wake you,' Sam protested when she questioned him.

'Where did you sleep then?'

'On the sofa.'

It bothered her that he was being so diligent. They shared breakfast, then headed into the country in Sam's rented four-wheel drive to view the two properties he had arranged to meet with their owners.

As they approached from the outside, the smooth adobe walls glowed apricot in the weak autumn sunshine, the buildings set comfortably into their natural surroundings. Indoors, the rooms were flooded with light from the lowering sun streaming in through south-facing windows.

Thick rammed earth walls provided thermal mass to collect the warmth now in winter but, for summer, ceiling fans were installed and windows would be opened to the breezes for cross-ventilation. Jennifer began to grasp the green concept of using solar energy and natural resources to power and warm homes. How much less strain on the environment and better for the planet. Such a pity Sam's voice was one of few in the architectural wilderness preaching the common sense of such a simple and easily implemented idea.

Again that evening, they quickly dined, Sam completely preoccupied and in a hurry to return to their room. Then he huddled to work over his laptop and they slept apart.

The following day they repeated the same visits to more welcoming people who opened up their homes, proud to share their experiences and knowledge.

Two days later, they took the hotel shuttle out to the airport and headed north on a flight to Phoenix in Arizona for a brief layover before continuing on to Walker Field in Grand Junction in the west of Colorado. Jennifer stepped from their small commuter flight and shrugged her coat collar tighter against the icy late afternoon wind, cutting in a sharp stinging blast across the airfield, and gazed around them.

'Stunning scenery,' she gasped, realising they were in a valley and taking in the backdrop of the southern slopes of the Grand Mesa she was to learn later was one of the largest flat-top mountains in the world.

'Sure is.' Sam gently took her elbow and guided them toward yet another hire vehicle. 'Lots of hiking, hunting and fishing in the heart of wine country,' he explained as they climbed into their car and turned on the heater for warmth.

For the following few nights, they stayed in a cosy country inn set in the middle of vineyards. They toured through more amazing homes, Sam taking notes and photographs and obsessing over every detail. They ate their way through some wonderful meals in the hotel and the historic downtown area, detouring through almost leafless vineyards on their way back into the city. Jennifer never ceased to be awed by the natural beauty of the mesa and red rock canyon landscape dusted with snow.

Despite spending their days together, there was something missing. One night, with Sam hunched over his laptop as usual and keying in his notes, a neglected Jennifer peeked over his shoulder and hugged him from behind. He barely responded and she filled with confusion.

'What time did you want to stop for dinner?' she asked.

'Not sure I can. Room service?' he muttered vaguely.

'Again?' Jennifer moaned. 'You should take a break,' she suggested tactfully, thinking a meal where they actually sat across the table together and conversed without the laptop between them would be nice. She knew Sam was dedicated, but he seemed to be pushing himself so much these days. And she privately questioned why.

'I think I'll head down to the dining room, then, and leave you to finish up.' She paused, waiting for him to object. 'Okay?'

He looked up. 'Are you sure?'

No. Jen smiled. 'Of course. See you in a while.'

She scooped up a scarf and her purse and quietly shut the door. Dining alone far from home when her man was just upstairs was disappointing. The food churned around in her mouth and she lost her appetite.

Jennifer worried and puzzled over Sam's disappointing indifference to her arrival. She could only draw the sad conclusion that he no longer felt the same spark as she did and it would be pointless to stay when he was so absorbed in his work. While in America, his zeal and search for the perfect house had escalated. He was manic in his obsession over details and she wondered it if didn't stem from a personal rather than a professional need. He worked long hours, constantly travelled and seemed to be driving himself to exhaustion, seeking something he hadn't yet found. But what?

In light of all her doubts, Jennifer admitted it seemed he might be better off without her here after all. The harsh truth was hurtful and she almost cracked. So, miserably, she made her decision.

With courage drawn from a second glass of one of the lovely locally grown and refreshing chardonnays, Jennifer let herself back into their room later to find Sam was in the shower. She felt cowardly but packed her suitcase while he was still in the bathroom. When he appeared soon after in the hotel robe, a towel covered his face as he dried his hair, so he didn't immediately notice her return and activity with clothes strewn about and case half packed.

Finally, he caught sight of her and

stopped. 'What are you doing?'

Knowing the moment for truth had arrived, Jennifer paused and sat on the bed. 'I didn't come all this way to be with you to feel like just another piece of baggage you're lugging around with you. Being an optional nomad isn't working for me. I'm sorry I intruded on your work. I've come at a bad time for you.' When Sam just stared, speechless, as though she was a stranger, she waved a hand vaguely toward her case. 'I'll take another room and leave you in peace to do your work and arrange a flight home tomorrow.'

'This is crazy,' he said sharply, scowling.

'We can catch up another time in Australia. Only if you want,' she added, small pieces of her heart and self-esteem breaking off as she spoke.

'What's all this really about, Jen?'

Realising he didn't have a clue, she let him have it. 'You fall asleep slumped over the laptop on the desk or stretch out exhausted on a couch. Do you even remember the last time you had a decent sleep in a bed?' Sam shook his head, clearly astounded by her outburst, so she pushed on. 'I understand this is an important work trip for you but, honestly? I think you're pushing yourself way too hard.'

'This research is necessary and important to me,' he explained.

'I know, but do you know *why*? What's so vital and urgent you have to achieve it all *now* on this one single trip? Can't there be others?' Dumbstruck, Sam just glared. 'Your dedication is admirable, but at such a pace and rush? You grab a few hours here and there; drive yourself to the limit every daylight hour. It's almost like you're punishing yourself. You'll end up ruining your health.'

He scoffed. 'You have it all wrong.'

'Do I?' she challenged softly. 'You're not the same man I knew in Bundilla.'

He glared at her as though she was some kind of alien. 'Time is short and precious, Jennifer. Life doesn't last. The time to do anything is *now*.'

His comment triggered an alert in Jennifer's mind. A hint of what might lie behind Sam's fixation. She wondered if she should tell him or let him work it out for himself. Sometimes cold hard experience was a better teacher than sermon. As Rachel had discovered.

'Fair enough. At this point, I can see the importance of your work and I certainly don't expect you to drop anything on my account — '

Sam scowled in frustration. 'I'm taking every principle from every house I visit. I'm building up a vital dossier of information. When I'm done, I'll be able to design the perfect house.'

She stilled. There was his problem. 'That's quite an ambition. And a challenge. Does it exist?'

'I'll *make* it possible.' His eyes sparkled with fervent light.

'A house is not just bricks and mortar, but the people who live inside.' Jennifer immediately thought of Grace's cottage. It wasn't about its grandeur or lack thereof, but the environment it generated for its occupants. 'I know it's corny, but I believe that home really is where the heart is.'

'I know that.' He impatiently brushed her comment aside. 'I also know I can create the perfect design.'

'Knowing you, you'll certainly try. You're devoting every ounce of yourself to the project and your tireless work is admirable. But at what cost?'

'You doubt me!' he snapped, brown eyes blazing, offended by her challenge.

Oh Lord, Jennifer thought, this was turning into a major disagreement. Would Sam see sense as she understood it, or was this the end for them?

'No,' she said more gently, 'But I question your reasons.' She tried to sound rational. 'Watching you since I've arrived, it's hard not to be worried about you.'

'I realise I haven't had the time to give you my full attention — '

'I don't want it. This isn't about me. I'm not some needy high maintenance female seeking attention. My concern is only for you. We don't always find a sense of purpose out in the world. Personal contentment comes from within.' He watched her while she closed her suitcase. 'Whatever it is you're seeking, Sam, I'm leaving you so you can get on with it.'

'Jen,' he said weakly.

Crushed that he hardly raised an objection, she held up a hand and moved toward the door, hauling her case. 'It's really all right, Sam. Maybe there'll be another time and place when we connect again. But clearly, it's not in New Mexico or Colorado.' She managed to pull off a wry smile and shrugged. 'I'd love to hear from you again sometime.' Generously, she added, 'I really hope you're successful with this project, Sam.'

She was so tempted to blather on and offer further unwanted opinions but resisted. Probably best he found his own way. Which could take time. The deepest hurt and biggest question hovering between them was whether or not his own awakening would include her in his life again. She prayed the importance of what they had shared back in Bundilla would eventually register with him.

For Jennifer, standing in the hotel doorway was like teetering on a precipice, not knowing if you would fall or not. Would Sam pull her back?

'Take care,' she whispered, aching that he just stood across the room staring at her, making no move to cross the distance or reach out to her or say goodbye. Somehow she knew pride and indignity over her criticism meant he would never beg her to stay.

* * *

When his hotel room door clicked shut as Jennifer quietly disappeared, Sam shook himself and wondered what the hell had just happened. Why would she come all this way and then leave? Originally he had invited her to travel with him, but she refused, then she suddenly appeared and now ended up stomping out in dissatisfaction.

All the same, the shocking reversal made him stop and think.

His time back in Bundilla, where he had shared so much love and so many confidences with her, now seemed like it had happened to someone else. Another couple. He felt detached from it all over here. When had it all gone wrong?

More to the point, what had changed? Still reeling from her quiet determined exit which he hadn't seen coming, he felt yet again like another person had deserted him. First, his mother had abandoned him. Granted, out of good intentions. Then Mel and Barbara dispatched him off to a private school when he was young. All his life, he had struggled with feeling rootless and adrift. Now Jennifer had just walked out too.

He thrust a hand through his hair in frustration and cursed, heading for the mini bar and a drink. The brandy worked its magic soon enough as it scalded down his throat while he paced the room.

Confused and wounded by Jennifer's words, he winced to recall the glitter of tears in her eyes, visible even from across the room despite those lovely wisps of blonde hair escaping about her anguished face. He had crushed the strongest urge to stride over, take her in his arms and hug her, but shock at her disapproval held him back. She made his ambition sound unprincipled and shameful, but how else was he to achieve his dream if not with passion? No one had spoken to him so honestly and bluntly in a long time. He frowned. Ever?

Feeling hot from the alcohol and stuffy heated room, Sam crossed to the balcony doors and flung them open. The icy night air hit him like a slap in the face and woke him up. In the still and magical winter night, a carpet of stars decorated the sky. Mesmerised, he stepped back inside to grab a sweater, shrugged it on and returned outside to lean his arms on the balcony railing. He felt like he had just regained consciousness after being knocked out. His mind cleared, as though the pristine night had given him clarity.

Not sure if it was the brandy or Jennifer's firm words, he took a moment to let everything slide, empty his mind and just *be*. To his shame, he realised it had been months since he'd bothered. Ever since meeting a certain blonde from Bundilla and learning his real identity. Was it a coincidence the two were connected?

Taking time to stop and force himself to think, Sam was surprised to still feel the frustrated rage of regret that he had not known Grace was his mother while she was still alive. Reflecting on Jennifer's accusations, a sneaky suspicion niggled his mind that, since finding out, maybe he had been running from the hurt, trying to escape his loss and the truth. Blinded to the big picture and what was important to him in his life.

He cursed, thumped a fist on the

railing and fought his buried hurt. It only took seconds to lose the battle. He hung his head, his shoulders shook and he finally gave in to months of long withheld pent up grief for his mother and father. What he had learned and what could never be. In his release of grief, Sam remembered his father's lines from one of his letters: *I left part of me behind* . . . Peter Charlton had not been afraid to express his feelings for Grace Evans.

Jennifer had taken a punt and travelled halfway across the world to be with him. Naturally surprised to see the beautiful sight of her again, he had fought being filled with love against his need to also give his heart and soul to finish his research here. He had selfishly made her wait and she had politely backed off to return home. How could he have been so heartless to the woman he loved?

When his sorrow eased with cleansing and he felt his inner burden slowly lift like an unwelcome weight from his shoulders, it was clear he couldn't do a damn thing about Grace and Peter's loss of each other so young and knowing them as parents in his own life, but he sure could remedy something else. He straightened and took a deep breath. Time to face his demons.

★ ★ ★

Standing at Jennifer's door, knocking, Sam's stomach churned. Would she even talk to him? He knocked again, harder and louder. Why wasn't she responding? He checked his wristwatch. It wasn't even midnight. He panicked, thinking he might have the wrong room and checked the number reception had given him.

He was about to lope off in disappointment when the lock clicked and the door opened just a crack, chained. If the matter hadn't been so damned serious, he would have laughed. As it was, despite his angst, he stifled a grin. The tumbled sight of Jennifer's long hair about her shoulders, her face scrunching up and squinting against the hall light, yawning, melted his heart. Even her flannelette pyjamas weren't a turn-off.

'Sam — ' came out in a disbelieving sleepy voice.

'I know it's late. Can we talk?'

'That's right, you don't ever sleep,' she grumbled. 'Some of us need a few hours, you know?'

'I could come back in the morning if you promise not to leave until I do.'

She let out a gasp of exasperation and the chain rattled as she unlatched it. 'Oh for heaven's sake, I'm awake now. But make it quick.'

She led him into her room and settled on the sofa, tucking up her feet and snuggling into a woollen throw. 'What is it? Some new revelation about your work?'

He winced. He probably deserved that. Astonished to confront this new positive woman, he sank a hand into his pocket and gave a nervous swallow. 'No.

A revelation about me.' He drew a weary hand across his face and began. 'Firstly, I apologise for not treating you better since you arrived.'

She glared at him for a long while then muttered grudgingly, 'Apology accepted.'

Well, it *was* late and he'd woken her up. He'd need to work a little harder. He hadn't given much thought to this encounter, trusting the words would just come. So he spoke from his heart. 'I have a few things I need to say. Might be an idea if you don't interrupt.'

She yawned. 'I'll try not to fall asleep.'

Ouch! 'I need you,' he blurted out. He wasn't ready to say the three more important words until he'd explained.

'No kidding,' she said wryly, unimpressed. 'Is this going to take long?'

Okay, he'd dig deeper. 'I know I've hardly given that impression lately because I've been so focused on my research, which you kindly took the trouble to point out to me.'

She arched her eyebrows as if to say *So?* but remained silent and watchful. Strange he'd never noticed before that Jennifer Hale could be such a scary woman. He figured at this point, judging by her attitude, she probably thought she had nothing to lose. He hoped to change her mind.

'So — I've done some thinking and re-evaluating.' She kept staring. Highly unsettling. 'You were right.'

He didn't expect *I told you so* and he didn't get it. That kind of malice wasn't in Jennifer's personality. Still shaken from finally releasing his recent grief, he found it doubly hard to now confide his deepest emotions as well. But if he could share with anyone, it would be this woman.

'It cut deeper than I realised when Mel and Barbara told me Grace was my mother just before she died. So much was happening, I dug a hole for my feelings and pushed them in. It got worse when I was going through the cottage and read Peter's letters back home and Grace's diaries to learn that my adoptive parents reneged on their promise to my mother to let me grow up and stay in Bundilla so she could be part of my life, if only from a distance. Because she was living gratuitously in their house and Mel and Barbara had control over me, it must have been an impossible situation for her. I'm not sure when I'll be able to forgive them.

'But meeting you was the kick I needed to get out of my ditch.' He paused. 'For the first time, I felt comfortable and fully trusting of someone. It's easy with you. Usually.' He grinned, thinking of their disagreement earlier tonight. 'You listen and you genuinely care.'

Jennifer's face softened a little and she wasn't dozing off as threatened. In fact, he had captured her full attention. Her gaze settled over him with respect and fondness.

Bolstered by that spark of encouragement, he said, 'In the upheaval of it all, I guess I started searching for an identity. A sense of place and roots.

Being an architect, I thought of my ideal and perfect home and what I wanted it to be. It helped me forget for a while but perhaps I did get a bit carried away.'

'You have that right, Sam. I'd never take that away. But instead of healing, I felt it was becoming destructive. It hurt to see you like that,' she admitted quietly, 'and it was even harder to point it out. Did I have the right? Would it destroy our relationship?'

Their gazes met.

'Has it?' Sam murmured.

'Time will tell.'

When Jennifer shrugged, the throw slipped off her shoulder. Sam took the liberty of stepping forward to gently replace it and sat on the edge of the sofa beside her.

'I think you're wrong,' he said. 'I believe in our hearts we both already know we have what Grace and Peter did. A true and lasting love.' Sam caught up Jennifer's hands. 'So deep it helps solve and overcome any obstacles in life. My parents' journey together was short but, God willing, ours will be longer. Whatever it brings, however long or short it is destined to be, I know in my heart we'll be all right. When you're beside me, Jen, you make me stronger.'

Long before Sam finished, Jennifer had straightened and moved closer, tears trickling down her rapt and shining face. 'Wow, that's the longest personal speech I've ever heard you give,' she said shakily, swiping at her wet cheeks.

Sam frowned in doubt. 'Is that good?'

She nodded. 'Awesome.'

'Grace and Peter were brave enough to fall in love during a war. Do you think you could stick with me a while longer?' He itched to say the three little words but he had an idea and abstained.

'Maybe.'

'I could just kidnap you and take you along but I have a favour to ask of you.'

Jennifer shrugged. 'Okay. Try me.'

'There's one last trip I'd like to make.'

Jennifer held up a hand. 'Honestly Sam, if it's another state and more green homes — '

Sam chuckled and shook his head. 'No, I'd like to invite you to accompany me on a personal journey. Since Grace's death and learning more about my father, I'd really like to visit his war grave in Terendak War Cemetery in Melaka. A sort of pilgrimage, if you like.'

'Oh.' She hesitated. 'Where on earth is that?'

'Malaysia.'

She tilted her head, thinking. 'Sounds like something maybe you need to do alone,' she suggested.

'True, but I've thought about it long and hard,' he said softly, 'and I'd prefer to share it with you. With Rose living in Grace's cottage now and you knowing Grace and Peter's story, I feel like you and your family are a part of my history, too. Please say you'll come with me? It would mean a lot.'

Sam watched Jennifer mulling over

her decision. If she refused, his plans were shot. There was much more at stake here.

Eventually, she nodded. 'Of course. I'd be honoured.'

'Peace?'

Her smile broke the last shreds of tension between them.

'Can I give you a hug?'

'Why not?' She grinned.

Because they were already comfortably close, it was simple for Sam to draw Jennifer into his arms. Where he knew she belonged. He made it last. Smelt her familiar fragrance, felt her warmth against him, her silky hair brush against his cheek.

As they parted, Jennifer asked, 'What about the homes you planned to visit?'

'I'll cancel.'

Jennifer pulled back in amazement. 'Really?'

'I'll reschedule for the spring.'

'Are you sure?' She frowned. 'I can't promise I'll come with you but I'll always be there for you.'

'Positive.' He pressed a finger to hush her lips. 'I think we've both waited long enough, don't you?'

Their kiss was long and lovely and healing.

'Scoot,' Jennifer grinned eventually, gently pushing him away. 'I need more sleep even if you don't.'

8

Before she settled for the night, it fleetingly crossed Jennifer's mind as to where exactly her life would be when she returned to Australia. Presumably back with her mother, because her relationship with Sam was still unresolved. He had still promised nothing, but at least she knew he still wanted her in his life. Maybe that journey he mentioned together was meant for a time in the future. At least they were reunited and more on the same page in their commitment to each other.

She had promised herself to take one day at a time, enjoy her love for Sam and expect nothing more; then she wouldn't be disappointed. But it was hard to detach herself from the deep bond they had formed and impossible to imagine her life without him again. She clung to hope and that at least she had him exclusively for the duration of their Malaysia trip.

As Sam drove their hire vehicle back out to Walker Field Airport two days later, rugged up in warm layers with the heater on, Jennifer reflected on the new closeness they had developed even in that short time. Yesterday, Sam had spent the morning cancelling his last few remaining work commitments and setting up a tentative schedule some months hence, then in the afternoon he arranged their four-hour flight to Los Angeles that included a one-hour layover in Phoenix.

She insisted on retaining her separate room. The emotional distance gave them space to refresh their relationship. In mutual relief, they discovered Sam's words proved correct and their love *had* survived. A heightened appreciation for each other unfolded — warm and magnified affection between them, revealed in small respectful ways.

After a rest night on the west coast at an airport hotel, Jennifer faced the interminable flight halfway back across the world again with calm resignation. This leg of their travels together was a vital milestone in Sam's life and she felt privileged to share it with him. She suspected it, too, would help in his healing process.

Although cocooned in business class comfort in her own sleeper seat, Jennifer would have loved to snuggle up against Sam instead.

Upon landing in Kuala Lumpur, they were flung into the steamy heat and noisy crowds of Malaysia. The opposite of Colorado deep in winter. They shared another luxury hotel suite and caught up on jet lag sleep. It was all very well, Jennifer thought, to enjoy the excitement of travelling, but she was beginning to yearn for home again and staying in one place. She had kept in constant contact with Rose but was beginning to miss Bundilla and her friends.

The humidity and rain forcibly made them lethargic, slowing their pace to holiday mode. Winding down after busy weeks and long flights, they swam in the hotel pool and browsed the teeming markets in the negligible relief of evening. Jennifer discovered fabric shops selling glorious pastel hand-painted florals and, after too many purchases, sauntered around wearing only a sarong, a big sunhat and leather sandals. Sam downsized to casual, too, in linen shirts and cargo shorts. The physical transition set her pulse racing. She couldn't keep her eyes off him and found herself even more deeply in love with the charismatic man. Especially now he had allowed her more attention.

On the day of the planned cemetery visit, they could have taken the local plentiful but crowded express buses south to the historic port city of Melaka, but in the sapping heat Sam opted for the convenience of a taxi instead.

On the journey, he grew quiet and reflective, staring out of the window at the lush and vigorous green countryside one associated with the tropics as they passed. Jennifer squeezed his hand and smiled her support to let him know she understood.

The cemetery lay in a hollow off the main road, situated inside a military base. It was completely hidden, and accessed by a narrow road leading directly to the gate. Stepping from the taxi, Sam asked their driver guide to wait and unfolded a plan of the cemetery he had downloaded and printed off the internet. They strolled slowly in the heat toward rows of headstones emblazoned with a cross or the insignia of the soldier's regiment.

'Some Australian and New Zealand casualties of the Vietnam war were flown to Terendak and buried here,' Sam told her quietly as they searched for the grave they had come to visit.

When they found it, Sam stiffened. Jennifer sought his hand, damp in the heat, but comforting she hoped. Knowing this was an emotional time for him on many levels, she discreetly gave him time and space to pay his own private respects to the father he never knew and casually sauntered off nearby, always keeping an eye on him in case he needed her.

He squatted down and she heard him talking in low tones for a while. The touching scene made her heart ache with compassion. When he rose and searched around for her, she smiled and joined him again. 'You all right?' she murmured.

He nodded. 'I thanked him for writing all those letters to my mother and told him I'd read them so I knew a little of what he went through and that I felt I knew him better for it. Dad gave his life for his country as so many others did, too. I wish I'd known him. But if Grace loved him, that's enough recommendation for me. I'd say he must have been a top bloke.'

'A gentleman digger.' Jennifer slipped her hand into his again in a gesture of supporting strength. 'I have a feeling I'll be back.' He glanced down at her and a surge of love swept through her at the warmth and admiration in his eyes.

'After dragging you all over the world, I say we deserve a few days off before heading home.'

Jennifer's whole body sagged with relief at the word *home*. 'Doing absolutely nothing?' Sam nodded. 'Promise?'

'Absolutely nothing.'

'What did you have in mind?' she asked as they strolled lethargically back to the taxi.

'There are some beach resorts at Port Dickson.'

They'd brought their luggage so, in the late afternoon, they sank willingly into their vehicle and headed the short distance up the coast to their destination.

Alighting later, Jennifer gasped at the sight. 'We're staying here?'

'Come on. Let's check in and chill.'

Half an hour later, having marvelled endlessly over their luxury water chalet on stilts above a crystal ocean with its open-sky bathroom and four-poster bed draped with net, Jennifer strolled hand-in-hand with Sam on a stretch of private white sandy beach lapped by lazy waves and ringed with secluding greenery.

'If it wasn't so steamy, I'd be so tempted to live here,' she quipped.

'It's certainly relaxing and special. And not a little romantic,' he grinned.

'Well chosen, Mr. Charlton.'

'I'd only ever want to share a heavenly hideaway like this with you.' His voice softened and he grew serious. Alerted to a subtle and more intimate change in his mood, Jennifer allowed herself to be pulled against him and thoroughly kissed, the warm ocean waters washing over their bare feet as they held each other and watched the sun set in a flaming orange sky.

'Rather a perfect spot for a honeymoon, isn't it?' Sam murmured.

Jennifer sighed wistfully. 'I imagine so.'

Then he was fossicking in the pocket of his beige linen slacks and produced a small square burgundy velvet box. Without taking his eyes from hers, he opened it and said, 'Jennifer Hale, my dearest heart, I love you. For all time.

Will you marry me here and now in Malaysia?'

Stunned by all that was happening and so fast, she melted at his choice of lovely words and dared glance at what was inside the telltale box nestled on ivory silk. The diamond ring sparkled in the golden twilight and looked very special.

'Oh Sam,' she whispered. 'It's gorgeous.'

'It's Grace's engagement ring from Peter.'

Jennifer released a long sigh of amazement and pressed a hand over her mouth. 'Oh, my.'

'Do you accept it?'

'Absolutely.' She laughed and flung her arms around his neck. 'I love you with all my heart, too, Sam Charlton,' she breathed before he smothered any possible further conversation with ravaging possessive kisses.

When he removed the ring from its niche, Jennifer said, 'Your hands are shaking.'

'I've never done this before and I

only plan to do it once, so I want to get it right.'

'Don't drop it in the sand. We'll never find it again,' she giggled.

But he held it firmly and, as he slid it along her finger, they both realised the significance of the family heirloom, its importance in their own lives and the memories it would forever hold in their hearts.

Jennifer held out her hand to catch the diamond sparkles and tried to imagine when Peter had given it to Grace. All the hopes and dreams contained in this tiny gold band encrusted with a row of diamonds . . . They would have been expecting a long life together, not that a war would snatch it away.

That night they dined by candlelight and eagerly chatted over plans for the simplest of tropical weddings the following week.

'Are you sure you don't want me to arrange for your mother and Rachel to come over and be here for the ceremony?'

'No,' Jennifer assured him. 'But thank you for asking. Gives us an excuse to celebrate again when we get back — ' She had been about to say 'home' but checked herself and said, 'To Australia.'

'Let's book the café and invite everyone we know,' Sam said.

So their celebratory meal at least was to be in Bundilla. Inspired by his suggestion and thrilled with relief, she added, 'And give Sue free rein with the menu. She'll have a ball and it will be a nice surprise.'

They made another toast, using any excuse for more sparkling wine on such a memorable night.

Six days later with a light balmy breeze playing about the ends of her long hair tucked with frangipani, floating free and natural over her shoulders, Jennifer walked slowly from their villa through the tropical gardens toward Sam. He stood in a magical dreamy location beneath a thatched pavilion in the centre of a waterlily-covered lagoon.

As she stepped in her glittery sandals

onto the bridge to reach him, his gaze fully embraced his bride in her pale blue silk wedding sarong covered with an embroidered lace body veil that streamed out into a train behind her.

They held hands and grinned at each other throughout the simple ceremony, whispered their endearing vows of love and commitment, and sealed their marriage with a long tender kiss.

Later they shuffled barefoot in the sand which, in their blissful state, passed for dancing in the silvery moonlight, swaying languorously to music drifting across to them from somewhere off in the distance.

'I could stay forever just like this,' Sam murmured against her hair. 'Let me know when you're ready to go home.'

With his timely question, Jennifer cautiously broached the question always on her mind. 'And where do you think that might be?' She had mentally prepared herself to live in the city, if that was what Sam's work dictated.

'Wherever we want it to be.'

He seemed flexible and unconcerned, so Jennifer's hopes rose. 'Melbourne?' she ventured, hardly daring to breathe, waiting for his answer.

Nestled in his arms, their heads touching, she couldn't see his expression but felt him shrug. 'It's always up for discussion, of course, but since I was banished to the city at an early age and have lived there ever since, it's time for a change. I'm thinking small town, build our own house, a few kids. Charming my mother-in-law Rose to babysit occasionally.'

Jennifer's heart soared in surprise and opened up like a tropical flower with love and joy. They would be living in Bundilla? Near her mother in Grace's cottage?

She stilled and drew back to glance up at her husband. 'Are you serious?'

He kissed her nose. 'Never more. We may have to squeeze in with Rose for a few months until our home is built. If she'll have us,' he chuckled.

'Are you kidding? She'll be euphoric.'

Jennifer grew reflective. 'How will you feel about living in Grace's cottage again for a while?'

'Fine.'

'No regrets about selling?'

He shook his head. 'I'll always feel closest to her there but that's only natural. It's where I have all my memories. Glad the house is staying in the family.'

Family. Jennifer sighed. The word evoked such a burst of joy inside her, she doubted there was space for any more happiness. But there was always room to be mistaken.

Their honeymoon was not only idyllic and blissful, a time to seal their love and commitment, cocooned in their own intimate fantasy world for two weeks; but its end that could have been tinged with nostalgia also meant going home to Bundilla and family celebrations. They had sent word ahead of their personal news and return date.

A taxi whisked them from Melbourne airport to Sam's luxury modern apartment where they caught their breath overnight. As her husband phoned an estate agent to place his property on the market at an alarming price and spent the following morning in his office in meetings catching up since his absence, Jennifer took the opportunity to shop and rode the tram down St. Kilda Road into the city.

They reunited for dinner at a Southbank restaurant on the river terrace boulevard with spectacular views over the city lit up for the night. Jennifer gasped at its quiet elegant ambience and worried that Sam might expect them to live like this. She had a much simpler life in mind.

Sam grinned at her uncertainty and said in warm reassurance, 'I wanted this to be a special memory.'

'My life has been special since the day I met you. Well, maybe not that very first time,' she laughed.

He leant closer and whispered in her ear as they were ushered to their table, 'After tonight, we settle down to life together. But don't be surprised if I whip you away for a weekend alone now and again.'

Jennifer appreciated the indulgence but was relieved to know that although Sam had trodden a more privileged path in life, he was a realist with both big feet planted firmly on the ground, a green campaigner with an eye to make his mark and influence the future of architecture.

★　★　★

Jennifer bubbled with impatience for the whole long trip home up country. Sam sat quiet and controlled beside her, often reaching across to smile and squeeze her hand. No words were necessary.

As they cruised into town along Main Street, Jennifer smiled to herself and sighed. As wonderful as her world travels with Sam had been — and presumably there would be other trips abroad in the future — it was sublime to be home. In Bundilla. With a husband.

The car slid to a stop at the kerb in front of Rose's cottage. Her mother, forewarned of their arrival time, must have been waiting; for almost immediately she stepped onto the front porch, beaming. Jennifer hurled herself from the car and crushed her in a mutual welcoming hug.

'I would say you've just had the best month of your life,' Rose said.

'Hard to beat,' Jennifer admitted.

She turned at Sam's approach and Rose greeted her new son-in-law with equal joy and grace. 'Welcome home, son. Your room is ready and we'll eat dinner as soon as you're both settled.'

Walking down the immaculate familiar hallway, the smell of food wafting to them from the kitchen, open fire blazing on this cool day toward summer's end as they entered the amazing rear living space that overlooked the garden, Jennifer and Sam exchanged a glance of pure bliss.

The following days were a whirlwind blur of catching up with everyone and booking Sue's Place for the wedding renewal dinner, giving the delighted chef free rein with the menu. Within days Jennifer returned to work at the café and legal office, planning to continue indefinitely at both. With Rose's approval, Sam set up his study in a spare bedroom. Jennifer returned to home-cooked meals at each day's end and afterwards huddled in excited chatter over scribbling and ideas and designs for the home they planned to build. Sam had scoped out a large bush block on the edge of town.

Invitations and emails were sent out to family and friends, and telephone calls made to those living further afield to reserve them for the special day a few weeks hence.

Jennifer's excitement mounted on the morning of the *big day*, as everyone had taken to calling it. To marry Sam privately in Malaysia had been memorable and romantic, but to be given the chance to renew their vows and share a second celebration with family and friends was the icing on the proverbial wedding cake.

And what a gorgeous culinary marvel Sue created: five tiers of cupcakes nestled in pastel papers, decorated with swirls of creamy icing and Sue's delicate handmade pastel sugar roses. Jennifer couldn't wait to see what food she produced for the reception meal. Nervous for many reasons, she hadn't eaten properly for days, fielding dark disapproving glances from her mother. Thank heavens the simple late-morning ceremony would be followed immediately by Sue's luncheon. She didn't think she could hold out until dinner.

'Eat all of it now,' Rose admonished gently as the three of them sat at the breakfast table. 'You need plenty of stamina today.'

How times had changed. Jennifer returned her soft smile. Once, she had been the caretaker. Now her mother had reverted to that role. Normally they all looked after themselves, but today it seemed the older woman was determined to spoil the newlyweds.

'Mel and Barbara still haven't replied to their invitation,' Jennifer reminded Sam quietly when Rose bustled off to wash dishes and tidy up.

He shrugged in resignation. 'I hand-delivered it and broke down some barriers. Maybe they couldn't decide what to do.'

'But if they don't — '

He pressed a finger gently against her lips. 'Hush. *C'est la vie.* These things take time.'

Jennifer frowned again. 'And Rachel's not home yet either.' It was her biggest disappointment as she grew both excited and anxious at her sister's promised return.

'She said she'd make it.'

'With Rachel,' she said wryly, 'you never know. She's certainly cutting it close. The ceremony is in three hours.'

And those hours simply flew.

Earlier, Jennifer knew, because she had peeked out to verify the weather,

Rose had roamed around her garden to pick the freshest of every available bloom and have them delivered to the café.

Sam and Jennifer decided to wear the same outfits as in Malaysia and her brother, Joshua, from Castlemaine had appeared the day before in his vintage Studebaker, offering to drive the happy couple to the renewal service in regal style. Her easygoing, equally blond brother had arrived early to drive them the short distance for the brief informal ceremony.

Jennifer anxiously paced the hallway, worrying where Rachel could possibly be and why Mel and Barbara had decided not to come. And then she heard a car door bang and a familiar voice outside. Her heart burst with joy and relief when her sister emerged through the front doorway and stood expectantly in the hallway.

'Rachel!' she squealed.

The young woman's eyes shone with animated spirit. She looked healthy, and her skin glowing with a light tan. Her once short spiky coloured hair was gone and dark wild waves swayed about her shoulders.

'Hey,' she replied uncertainly.

Jennifer beamed and closed the distance between them for a hug. 'Rachel's here!' she yelled.

Everyone rushed into the hallway. Rose hugged her daughter, Sam his new sister-in-law. Joshua grinned and lightly punched her on the arm.

'We've been so worried about you,' Jennifer said.

'Really?'

'Of course. What happened?'

Rachel crinkled her nose. 'My car broke down.'

'You drove all the way down?'

She nodded. 'I picked up a two-door hatchback. It's seen better days but it was doing fine until thirty minutes out when something started clunking and she stopped. I phoned the RACV and they came out to help.'

'You should have phoned us,' Rose fussed.

'I didn't want to bother anyone. I knew you'd all be busy getting ready for the ceremony.'

'Very thoughtful of you, dear, but we wouldn't have minded a bit. Joshua was free. He's been our odd-job man all morning.'

'Well, I'm here now,' she said breezily, all traces gone of the sullen unhappy person she had been when she left six months before.

'Where's your car now, then?' Sam asked.

'It's been towed to George's garage.'

Relief washed through Jennifer and tears pooled in her eyes at the sight of her happy little sister.

'Heavens, no tears. You'll ruin your mascara.' Rachel glanced down at her denim shorts and T-shirt. 'The bride and groom look ready to leave so I guess I don't have time to change.'

'You're absolutely lovely as you are, but we'll wait.'

'Are you sure?' Jennifer nodded. Rachel hesitated but only for a split second. 'I bought a new dress especially.'

'Then go.' Jennifer gently thrust her toward the bedroom. 'You're coming with us, aren't you, Mum? Josh, there's room.'

Rose cast a shy smile toward them. 'Don't worry about me, dear. I have a ride.'

'Oh?'

They hadn't discussed it, but Jennifer had assumed the three of them would take the short ride to the café together. Her mother hadn't mentioned any alternative plans.

'Someone coming to get you?' Jennifer had her back to the front door.

Rose peered over her shoulder. 'Yes, and I believe he's here now.'

He? Jennifer whirled around in unison with everyone else, staring through the lush front garden shrubbery to see the shiny long black nose of an identifiable and distinguished classic Jaguar coupé glide into the kerb.

Smiling benignly at her speechless audience, Rose trotted calmly down the hallway. 'Don't look so alarmed. We're just good friends. See you all at the café.'

By then, Stewart Dalton was opening the front door, waving to his gaping onlookers and offering an arm in escort to his lady passenger. Jennifer recalled his casual comment before she had left for America to see Sam that he would keep an eye on her mother while she was away. She wondered just how much attention Rose had been receiving. She shook her head in amazement, too speechless to say anything to either Sam or Joshua when Rachel reappeared.

Joshua whistled softly. 'Nice.'

'It's not too much?' She looked down anxiously at her fitted floral dress in shades of peach and green, the soft colours drawing out her hidden beauty. She clutched a matching bag and her feet were tucked into chunky stylish black heels. Her freshly brushed hair swung softly about her lightly made-up face.

'Rachel,' Jennifer murmured in admiration, 'you look gorgeous.' She couldn't recall the last time she'd ever seen her in a dress. Her femininity was usually hidden beneath tight shabby jeans.

'You can ride with us,' Jennifer offered.

'No, I'll walk.' She started down the hallway, half turning to field further objections. 'It's okay, really. I need some peace to catch my breath.'

Jennifer understood. Her sister was becoming her own person. 'Of course you do. Don't hurry. We'll drive around the block. Can you walk in those?' she nodded to her high heels.

Rachel smiled and nodded. 'They're more comfortable than they look.' She hesitated with one hand on the front door. 'Jennifer? You look absolutely beautiful. I wouldn't have missed this for anything.' Her brow dipped into a quick frown. 'Sam, find her a tissue. She's going to cry.'

She waved and was gone. Sam hugged his wife for a moment until her emotions subsided. Joshua gave them privacy and waited in the car. Ten minutes later they stepped out of their bridal vehicle and across the cafe threshold.

There was no competition, of course. Vicar David was the only option for celebrant. Jennifer could have asked her brother, Luke, but he was not fully trained yet. In a way, she was relieved because David had been the glue that held her together emotionally this past year and he would always be her best mate. He stood now in front of the unlit café fireplace, beaming across the room decorated with chains of streamers looped overhead, their guests already seated at tables. Jennifer gasped to see Mel and Barbara toward the back. She squeezed Sam's hand tight and he smiled.

They wove their way toward David, a deep thrill giving Jennifer a buzz of adrenaline that remained with her throughout the day.

'Mr. and Mrs. Charlton,' David began, and the brief renewal service was underway. Jennifer imagined the surprise for many to hear the unfamiliar name.

Afterward, confetti fluttered over them from every direction. She and Sam were gripped in loving hugs from all sides as laughter and loud chatter filled the room. Everyone dear to them had come.

After the ceremony and before dinner, Sam and Jennifer moved among their guests, trying to personally catch up with everyone.

'Thank you for choosing me to do the honours,' David said to them immediately after the ceremony. 'I hope you'll have me again to do all your future christenings.'

'David!' Jennifer blushed and nudged him firmly, embarrassed because Sam was standing close beside her with an arm about her waist and must have overheard.

'Sounds like a plan to me.'

First in line with congratulations was Rose. 'You look absolutely stunning, my dear. I wish you life's richest blessings and happiness.' She hugged them both.

'Your mother's sentiments are mine, too, Jennifer.' Stewart Dalton was at her side, dapper in a grey pinstriped suit and cheeky red bow tie. 'Like it?' he chuckled.

'Most dashing.' More hugs.

Then her oldest brother Adam pressed forward and caught her hands. 'Stunning, sis. Well done.' They hugged and kissed and he shook hands with Sam.

'Thank you for coming all the way from outback Queensland. I want to get family photos while we're all together.'

Adam — tall, tanned and gorgeous, always the most confident of her brothers — drew every woman's attention in the room and was soon whisked away.

'Joshua and Stewart have their heads together already,' Jennifer said. 'Probably talking about old cars.' She laughed.

Her youngest brother, quiet Luke, hovered in the background all day.

'Doesn't look as though he's enjoying

himself,' Sam murmured in her ear following the direction of her glance.

'He's conservative, that's all. Needs a good lively woman to loosen him up.'

Then Jennifer was finally introduced by Sam to his uncle William Evans, Grace's brother. She knew he had found them still on the family farm in Shepparton and had made telephone and letter contact since, but this was their first meeting in person. William had been naturally shocked to learn of his sister's death belatedly. By the time he had learnt of his existence through Grace's diaries, Sam was furious that Mel and Barbara had not bothered to find him and let him know, since he and his family were her only living relations. As a result, Sam was determined to redress the oversight. In the meantime, Sam had exchanged photographs with his aunt and uncle.

As they approached each other in a corner of the café, Jennifer was unfairly disappointed that balding and trim William Evans did not favour Grace more. Until he smiled. Then his face so resembled his sister's photograph, it took her breath away. Beside her, Sam stared.

'Son.' William reached out and shook his hand. 'We are so pleased to have the privilege to finally meet you.'

Sam, appearing to compose himself at this emotional moment, said simply, 'Uncle William. I'm overwhelmed.'

'Same as us, lad. Same as us. Thank you for letting us know about our Gracie.' Jennifer smiled at the touching endearment. 'And for inviting us here today to share in such a wonderful day and meet you. Speaking of us . . . ' he said, turning to the homely woman beside him, smiling at her tenderly and placing an arm around her shoulder.

This is what I want, Jennifer thought. This is what I shall have. A lifetime with my man. Had Grace and Peter been allowed a life together, their love would have endured as well, she was certain.

'This is my wife, May.'

'Auntie May.' Sam greeted her

warmly and favoured her with a kiss on the cheek.

'Samuel.' She regarded him thought-fully, still clutching his hands tight. 'You are so like your mother. You will keep Grace alive for us.'

Jennifer whipped a side glance to her husband and watched him fill with pride.

'I wish I'd known her better.'

'We can soon sort that out,' May said firmly. 'William has inherited all the old family photograph albums. I know you invited all our family as a group, but we have three sons and a daughter, all married with children,' May put in proudly, beaming. 'We didn't want to overwhelm you on your special day,' she chuckled.

'I can't wait to meet them all,' Sam assured her.

'You both have an open invitation any time to come up to the farm.' William's friendly glance included Jennifer. 'You can take your time to meet your cousins and their spouses, and all your nieces and nephews. Learn about your family history. Your grandparents Edward and Bessie.' His gaze clouded. 'Hard people. Strict,' he admitted, frowning and shaking his head. 'My heart broke when they turned Gracie away but we secretly kept in touch, as you know. Even met once or twice over the years,' he reflected. 'But she still felt guilty, even after our parents died. Never really lost her sense of shame, so she stayed a very private person. Looking at you, Sam, my lad, she'd every right to be so proud. She sent us your photograph when you were a boy. Not so many in recent years. From what we see here today, you've grown into a fine upstanding man. We're both so proud to welcome you into the family.'

Jennifer could see Sam was swamped with happy emotion, so to help him out and cover his silence, she said quickly, 'We'll definitely come up for a visit as soon as we can arrange it.'

'I hope you like fishing, lad, because we camp up on the Murray River and angle for the great Murray cod,' he laughed.

'I've never fished in my life,' Sam admitted, recovering. 'But I look forward to having you teach me.'

They parted, promising to keep in touch and catch up soon.

Then Sue appeared, flushed and smiling from the kitchen, to signal dinner. As one indulgent course after another appeared, from delicately prepared appetisers to the roast pork and crackling with roasted summer vegetables, platters continued to arrive until Jennifer's appetite was more than sated. Champagne flowed, glowing toasts and speeches were made, then followed the crowning desserts; pavlovas laden with berries and the cupcake tower were mysteriously reduced by half.

In a rare idle moment during the afternoon, Jennifer's gaze scanned the room. She noticed Tim Parker, Sue's lanky cheerful son not yet back at university, chatting animatedly to Rachel, looking captivated. Maybe he was endorsing the benefits of higher education. They certainly seemed absorbed in conversation.

Later, Jennifer grabbed a moment to speak with her sister when she caught her eye across the buzzing room, raised her brows in query and beckoned. Rachel nodded and wove between tables to join her.

'I'm so sorry we haven't had a chance yet to talk,' Jennifer apologised.

'That's okay.' She glanced around. 'I'm actually having a great time.' She sounded surprised. 'Small towns aren't usually my thing. I think I'm seeing everyone through different eyes today.'

'I'm so relieved you finally arrived safely. How long can you stay?'

Rachel shrugged. 'Depends on a few things.'

Jennifer didn't pry or push. Her bubbly sister had matured so much even in the months since they had been apart. 'So, tell me all your news and what you're doing now.' Jennifer decided to be tactful and concentrate on her life since Boomer.

'Still working at the beach café.' She pulled a wry grin. 'In hospitality, can you believe it? Just like you. Something I swore I would never do. I try to work extra weekend and late shifts so the pay's better.'

Her little sister appreciated the value of a dollar now, it seemed. She smiled to herself. 'You're staying up there, then?'

She nodded. 'There's this guy comes into the café most days with this cool iPad. He has wi fi on it and everything. I asked him what he did one day and he said he's a journalist.' Excitement glittered in her dark eyes. 'I told him I'd only ever written a diary.'

'You do?'

Rachel wriggled uncomfortably. 'I saw this counsellor for a while after Boomer split. I was a mess,' she admitted in a small voice. 'So she recommended I record my feelings.'

'Oh, honey.' Jennifer reached out and squeezed her hands. 'I wish I'd been there for you.'

'No drama,' she said matter-of-factly. 'Made me stand on my own two feet. Anyway, this guy says that a diary can be not only therapy but produce good stuff. I told him mine was detailed but basically drivel. Then you know what? He challenged me to write something. Anything from my life. And show it to him.'

'And did you?'

'I asked him why and he said he freelances for the Brisbane *Courier Mail* and other big city newspapers all over the country. He said if I was any good, he'd tell me.'

Jennifer waited. 'And?'

'He liked it. Said it was raw but I had potential.'

'Sounds encouraging.'

'So . . . I was thinking . . . maybe I could try some communications and journalism units. See how I go, you know?'

'Great.' Jennifer was quietly ecstatic for her sister. 'Where would you study?'

'Open University on the internet so I can keep working. I want to travel, Jen.

There's so much to see out in the world once you start looking,' she enthused. 'I could write about it. Work while I was having some adventures.'

'Sounds like an exciting plan to me.'

'Yeah.' Rachel beamed. 'I'll enrol when I get back.'

'Well, we must make the most of it while you're here, then. Mum will love having you home for a while. The boys can only stay a few days before they have to get back for work, too.'

Then John and Tim Parker pushed back and rearranged the tables, since few people were seated at them now anyway, and music started. Slow clapping began and 'Dance, dance,' was called out, the guests all shouting in Jennifer and Sam's direction.

Smiling delightedly at each other, they moved out onto the floor, followed moments later by Stewart and Rose, then William and May. The young ones chose to remain on the sidelines, indulgently nudging one another at the slow traditional dancing of their elders.

But they couldn't contain their eagerness for long; the music grew louder and lively as they bopped around, leaving only the most energetic remaining while everyone else retired for a break.

In the lull, and because so far Mel and Barbara appeared reluctant to make any move toward them, Jennifer leaned closer to Sam so he could hear above the music, and nodded in their direction.

'I think it's time, don't you?'

'I guess someone has to make the first move.'

'Honestly, Sam, Barbara looks like she's sucked a lemon. It's obvious she only came today out of duty and for appearances. Why did she bother if she's not happy for us?' Jennifer tried not to let their lack of participation spoil this day, although their restraint had subconsciously bothered her more than she would confess.

'Time to invade their personal space. I suspect they're holding back because they're unsure.'

Barbara visibly tensed as they approached, and Mel knocked back the last of his beer.

'We're pleased you came,' Sam said warmly to break the ice.

'Are you?' Barbara said crisply. Mel shot her a glance of disapproval.

'Yes, we are. I think it's time we all buried the hatchet,' Sam declared. 'Preferably not in each other.'

Mel gave an appreciative chuckle but stilted, if any, conversation was offered in return and an uncomfortable silence followed.

'William and May Evans are here, as you will have seen, but they're leaving first thing tomorrow. It might be a nice gesture if you make yourself known to them,' Sam suggested, trying to break down the wall.

No response except for polite smiles and a grunt from Mel.

'We hope you've been able to enjoy the day. It was important to us to have all our families here,' Jennifer offered, sensing tension and reticence flow from

Barbara more than Mel. 'It's not often my whole family can get together. My sister and brothers are all here. Makes for quite a reunion.'

She was babbling with nerves, but my goodness this was hard work and reconciliation would take time. Granted, they'd had much to cope with. Losing the respect of a son. Suddenly gaining an unsuitable daughter-in-law. Knowing she didn't measure up to Barbara's social standards, Jennifer had decided there was little else they could do until the older couple accepted the situation and thawed.

Sam had taken what must have been a difficult first step for him when he personally delivered their invitation to Melrose Park. He had apparently apologised for his outburst but returned to Grace's cottage gutted, believing their chilly wariness and limited response meant he was not forgiven.

All Jennifer could do was hold and comfort him, trusting they softened with time, acknowledging all parties had been

316

in the wrong. Perhaps Sam's truths had shaken them up harder then he realised. But his attempt at mending fences had so far proved useless. He blamed himself, Jennifer knew, for speaking so strongly and honestly to them, but the deed was done. Past. All secrets had been revealed, and they both believed life for everyone should now be about moving on and looking to the future.

Frustrated, Jennifer backed away and smiled directly at Barbara in challenge. She suspected she would never be regarded as good enough in the other woman's eyes, but she was determined to simply be herself and make an effort. Civility cost nothing. 'We must catch up for dinner some time,' she said brightly, then threw the ball into their arena, adding generously, 'Perhaps you can let us know when you both have time and it suits.'

Sam's quick glance down at her told her he could have eaten her with gratitude. Jennifer returned his warm gaze with a shrug that said *What more can we do?*

Mel shuffled, hands sunk into his trouser pockets, and rocked on his heels. 'I'll check my diary. Maybe we can arrange something.'

'We look forward to it.' Sam paused before continuing, 'You know, we've bought a bush block out your way. You might be interested to come out and take a look. Lot 150 on Old Coach Road.'

Mel tried to look casual but Jennifer noted his attention sharpen. 'Might get a moment to drive past.'

'I have some challenging building methods you might care to consider. If your company is interested to quote for its construction, of course.'

Jennifer wanted to punch the air with joy at even such a small breakthrough. Barbara was another matter. She struggled to think what on earth she and Sam could both do to make her happier and be prepared to include them in her life.

As they moved away, Barbara finally spoke. 'Jennifer?' she said softly. There was the longest pause, during which

Jennifer could see her wrestling for words. 'You look just lovely today.'

A stunned Jennifer said simply, 'Thank you,' and almost burst into tears with relief. The first tiny step.

★ ★ ★

In the end, the secret path to Barbara's heart emerged gradually with the arrival of twins, Peter and little Gracie Charlton, two years later. Perhaps she had learned by watching Rose on the occasional family gatherings; she was a natural grandmother whose front door and arms were always open when the toddlers scampered up her front path, no matter that their tiny feet crushed the odd flower or two, or a bloom was plucked from its stem and held up as a gift for Grandma Rose.

When her mother lovingly complained about being overrun, Jennifer laughed and said, 'Better catch your breath, Grandma; I'm planning on having a dozen until we use up all the family names.' Her tummy was already swollen with the twins' baby sister, to be called Rosie.

For Barbara, grandchildren meant a second chance. An opportunity to redress the imbalance. Jennifer and Sam witnessed the deep delight the young lives brought to her. The refreshing spark when small feet pattered through the big rooms of Melville Park and short arms reached out to be picked up.

Mel sent out hints for *the boy's education*.

'What about Gracie? Do you have a private school in mind for her, too?' Jennifer teased.

In fact, she had no intention of parting with her precious children and Sam had strict ideas himself about keeping his offspring close. They both agreed the next generation of Charltons would be schooled in Bundilla. The time would come when they were old enough to leave home of their own accord; but for now, that time was too far distant to consider.

Mel and Sam slowly eased into a comfortable and informal partnership of sorts, working together designing and building green environmental homes. Toys invariably littered Sam's study floor, two chatty children interrupting their father.

Their family home, built by the Keats Construction Company, was a work in progress, Sam always changing his mind and adapting or extending something. The staircase landing flooded with light dancing in rainbow reflections from a Gothic stained glass window. French windows opened onto sweeping lawns. Young trees would grow with the children of the house and rope swings dangle from their branches, puppies chasing them across the sweet-smelling freshly mown grass.

'Ah, the perfect home,' Jennifer said wryly one day, glancing across at her husband with a mischievous grin.

Sam threw back his head and gave a hearty laugh of appreciation at her ironic words. They both knew now that,

although their home may not be perfect, and they wouldn't necessarily want
it to be, they would work hand-in-hand
to make it a place of love and harmony
and laughter.

'Perfect?' he challenged, grinning.

'Perfect for us!'

THE END